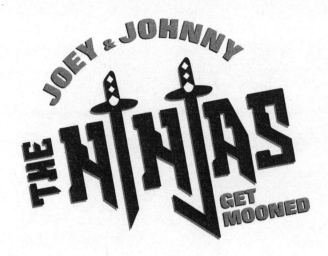

Kevin Serwacki

Chris Pallace

BALZER + BRAY

An Imprint of HarperCollins*Publishers*

Balzer + Bray is an imprint of HarperCollins Publishers.

Joey and Johnny, the Ninjas: Get Mooned
Library of Congress Cataloging-in-Publication Data
Serwacki.
 Get mooned / Kevin Serwacki, Chris Pallace. — First edition.
  pages cm. — (Joey and Johnny, the ninjas)
 Summary: "Best friends and ninjas-in-training Joey and Johnny are sent on a
special mission to investigate their rival ninja school's use of advanced technological
weapons"— Provided by publisher.
 ISBN 978-0-06-229933-8 (hardcover)
 [1. Ninjas—Fiction. 2. Schools—Fiction. 3. Best friends—Fiction. 4. Friendship—
Fiction. 5. Technology—Fiction. 6. Competition (Psychology)—Fiction.
7. Humorous stories.] I. Pallace, Chris. II. Title.
PZ7.S4886Get 2015   2014010016
[Fic]—dc23   CIP
                                                                              AC
15 16 17 18 19 CG/RRDH 10 9 8 7 6 5 4 3 2 1

First Edition

Dedicated to the patience of my parents,
Matt and Vee;
the tenacity of my agent, Abi;
the faith of our editor, Donna;
and the very strange foresight
of the nine-year-old version of me.
—K.S.

For Rogan and Tina, who convinced me I could.
—C.P.

THE DEATH OF JOEY AND JOHNNY

In which the boys probably
do not make it to Chapter Two.

"**W**ell, this is the end for us, my stalwart friend Johnny! Together we face a glittering sea of sharpened steel that will engulf us both. Know this, you villainous hordes, though I, *Joey*, shall dispatch hundreds—*nay, thousands*—of you before I expire, those of you who survive shall have the noble honor of telling the last of our exalted exploits! And now the call to arms! We rush forth unto doom's bosom! Chop! Slice! And alas, I fall! Fall . . . fall . . ."

"Um . . . Johnny? Did you have anything you wanted to say?" Joey asked.

"Pancakes!" said Johnny. "I'm going to miss them . . .

A *lot*! I mean, a whole bunch!"

"Okay, boys, you can stop now."

Joey and Johnny froze in the middle of their death throes.

Master Renbow adjusted the cuffs of his robes and swished to the front of the classroom. "Joey, good effort! It could use a little editing. Try to say more with less. Remember, Blademaster Steel Bloodsport's famous last words were 'My *heart*!' You don't have to be quite so succinct, but time is often an issue in these situations. I'm calling that a B minus." He recorded the grade with a long, sparkly pen using big, loopy flourishes that managed to involve his whole body.

Joey looked stricken. "Yes, Master Renbow," he said, and sat down with hunched shoulders.

"Now, Johnny," said Master Renbow, rubbing his forehead as he regarded his student. A lot of people rubbed their foreheads while talking to Johnny, so many that Johnny began to recognize it as a sign that someone was about to talk to him.

"*Pancakes*, Johnny?" Their sensei gave a long sigh before finally adding, "It needs work."

Johnny sat down. He was the only student who had a dooley-bopper sprouting from the top of his ninja mask. While his face didn't register the slightest emotion at his teacher's words, the dooley-bopper drooped slightly, making him look disappointed.

Master Renbow carefully pulled his long sleeves out of the way as he walked to the board and picked up the chalk. There were times when it was a curse to wear so much black. "Class, your final words before dying are *very* important, you don't want to wait until the last minute to get them right!"

With squeaking strokes he wrote, "Gah! My shoe! Bloooorg," and said, "Anyone recognize *these* immortal words?"

A small ninja named Ting raised his hand to about half-mast. Ting was not known to do anything at full-mast. "Sir, they are Shogun Wraithblade's last words?"

"Yes," said Renbow. "Your death is already going to be violent and painful—why should it be embarrassing too?"

A flaming arrow thunked into the wall beside Renbow's head. He pushed his glasses back on his nose to get a good look at it. "I really question the need for these arrows to be on fire," he muttered as he unrolled the small scroll tied to it. "Joey! Johnny! Headmaster

FangSwan wishes to see you in his office immediately. Ting, get some water, the tapestries are burning."

As the two students left and the classroom burned, their sensei attempted to restore order.

"Okay, who's ready to die next? Brad? Show them how it's done."

At this point you might be wondering who's telling you this story. Who would have the lowdown on all things ninja? Well, that would be me, the Wiseman. Technically "a" wiseman: it's more of a job title than a name, but I am one of the best, if I do say so myself.

Not all wisemen and wisewomen are created equal, and some barely deserve the name. Dillydale Fwops was famous for being the dumbest wiseman who ever lived. He was known for answering questions by throwing himself down a well, or wearing a bucket for three days. While a few will argue that he was just too wise for anyone to understand, I know *my* opinion on it.

We get assigned to locations based on our capacity for wisdom. For example: if you live in a goat-herding village at the butt end of the world, then, chances are, you'll have a wiseman to match. Now, give the man his due: for all goat- and goat-milk-related questions, you won't find a higher authority, and he probably even knows a thing or two about yaks. I'm just suggesting that you might want to hold off on asking the big stuff, unless you want a heavily goat-laden metaphor for your answer.

By comparison, the only thing I don't know is what I don't know. I am the wiseman for Lemming Falls and its surrounding territories. That means I have to keep up-to-date on all its peoples, creatures, scientific discoveries, mystic lore, and anything else someone might have a question about. It's a big job. On top of the normal wiseman stuff, I've had to study up on pocket dimensions and the difference between a haiku and a hikyu.

Lemming Falls is home to a thriving superhero community, a number of indigenous cryptozoological beasties, and—of course—ninjas. There are also rumors of Sky Pirates, but I'm probably getting ahead of myself. Point is, I know something about everything, and what I don't know, I'll make up and you'll never know. I'm just that good.

We wisemen are found in lots of places, but you won't find us unless you're willing to work for it. We'll perch at the tops of impossible-to-climb mountains, or deep underground in lost tombs. If we weren't so difficult to get to, everyone would be constantly bugging us to bestow our wisdom upon them, and who needs that? Looking for a solution to the inner turmoil of your soul? Seek out a wiseman. I am not here to help you find your keys.

Anyway, enough about me. It's lovely to meet you. Now on with the story.

Kick Foot Academy is the world's premier ninja school and its students, known as "Kick Foots," are the very best ninjas. Anyone who says otherwise will have to face its headmaster, FangSwan. So no one says otherwise.

In much the same way that hurricanes are given names like "Irene" or "Gladys," FangSwan's epic temper tantrums are also named. Like "the one about the potatoes" or "the one about the nose-whistling." It's getting more and more difficult to find any subject matter that can't be tied to a volcanic outburst from KFA's undisputed leader.

In a particularly famous incident, Headmaster FangSwan was invited to a gala performance of the famous ballet *Swan Lake*. The promoters thought he would be particularly enchanted by the occurrence of the word "swan" in both their names.

During the performance, a hapless ballerina lost control of her shoe, and it made the questionable decision to direct itself toward the headmaster's face. With a twist of his wrist, FangSwan returned the shoe to the ballerina's foot with such force that the dancer spun for the rest of the ballet and well into the next day. Upon leaving the theater, FangSwan wrote on a comment card, "Thank you for the lovely performance. The assassination attempt was particularly pleasing to me."

This is what FangSwan did to a ballerina with a loose shoe. Imagine what he might do with Joey and Johnny, wayward students at his school, at whose heels trouble and embarrassment followed like dumb loyal dogs. The honor of FangSwan's school was his most precious concern, and there was no reasonable way to tell what he'd consider a killing offense.

No Kick Foot Academy student had ever left FangSwan's office smiling or carrying a balloon. In fact, no student in anyone's memory had ever actually walked out of FangSwan's office. Students had certainly gone in and there were sometimes student-shaped holes in the door, floor, or ceiling to show that they had left, but it was generally understood that Headmaster FangSwan didn't meet with you unless you were deeply in trouble.

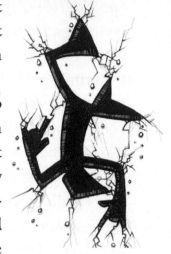

There are some headmasters who might invite a student in to pass on a kind word or give a reassuring pat on the back. FangSwan didn't know how to pat, and kind words were generally saved for particularly skilled enemies just before he delivered the killing blow. For Joey and Johnny, they were off to face the headsman.

Johnny rested his hand on his terrified friend's shoulder as they left the classroom. "Well, I think our performance went down pretty well!"

"Did you not read the last paragraph *or* the chapter heading? We're off to face our doom!"

"But our last day on earth is *also* the day our theater master covered last dying words! I mean, what are the chances? How lucky are *we*?"

"Johnny, I'm not going out on B-minus last words. Maybe if we can figure out what it was we did, we can craft a suitable apology."

"That's true—FangSwan is famous for his acts of forgiveness."

"Okay, well, we have three long hallways, two staircases, and the Hall of Accusation to go before we get to his office. That's all the time we have to figure it out," said Joey. "I think it was that angry Oni you let loose in the library."

"I didn't let him loose!" cried Johnny, looking hurt. "He just followed me in there after I helped pull that nasty thorn out of his face!"

Joey did the forehead rub. "That wasn't a thorn, Johnny, that was his tusk."

"And think about how much damage he did to the library afterward. The entire N section is gone! It's actually kinda lucky he didn't have that second tusk. It could've been twice as bad."

The point was debatable, but Joey decided this was not the time. They both went silent as their steps counted down their life spans. They'd already reached the end of the first hallway.

"Anyway," continued Johnny, "I'm pretty sure it was you and the pee incident."

Joey stopped dead. "Gah! Wuh? There was no pee incident!"

"Yes, there was, Joey! Remember that pee rolled off your spoon and we lost the east wing of the cafeteria?"

"Oh, *pea*!" said Joey with relief. "The *pea* that rolled off my spoon!"

"Yes, pea! Oh, did I say 'pee'? No, I meant 'pea.'"

To be fair, the pea in question had been a centuries-old magic object. It had been created by a sorcerer named Calamideas who began every day with "Hey, wouldn't it be funny if . . ." In this case he'd jinxed the pea to become eight thousand times larger if it should ever touch the ground. For years it had been buried deep in the school's bottomless vaults. But the problem with trying to hide dangerous things in a school for ninjas is that breaking into impossible vaults often counts as extra credit. A student looking to turn his B plus into an A threw the pea into a chicken potpie, and from there it found itself badly balanced on Joey's spoon.

"Well, that was hardly my fault!" Joey exclaimed, then added with hope, "I'm sure FangSwan couldn't blame me for that."

WISEMAN NOTE: Self-delusion is a force more powerful than any punch.

Joey slowed his pace. Their echoing footfalls were suddenly precious to his ears. When had dust motes ever looked so beautiful? Why hadn't he appreciated the smell of flowers more? Why was he thinking about flowers? Ah! Was that a bird? A sweet bird that probably had years more of its life left to live! "Curse you and your stupid long life, you stupid bird!"

A shadow fell over the bird, and it disappeared in midflutter.

Joey stared at the spot where it had been. "Johnny, I think I just cursed a bird to death!"

Johnny looked upset for the first time all day. "Why would you do that?"

"I didn't *know* I could do that!" said Joey, looking at his own hands as if they might start shooting lightning.

Someone coughed behind them, making them spin and flail.

"WAH!" said Joey.

"Dog puppets!" said Johnny.

A small girl with hair like a giant ninja star was standing behind them, way too close, holding the bird in her hands. It looked ruffled but unhurt.

"*Peoni!*" cried the boys.

"You guys didn't hear my heartbeat *or* sense a change in the air," she said with a little satisfied smile. "Face it! I snuck up on you!" She took her finger and got it as close to Joey's forehead as she could without actually touching him. "IIIIIIII snuck up on yooooooooouuu!" This was accompanied by a little dance.

WISEMAN NOTE: Sneaking up on a ninja is like catching your buddy with a finger up his nose. It's an accomplishment, but it won't be appreciated.

"I *smelled* you, Peoni!" Joey said while trying to whack her finger away. "Anyway, why did you attack that bird?"

She looked momentarily worried as she took a quick sniff of her shirt. "I didn't attack the bird! He's been sick and I've been taking care of him for the past six weeks, but he managed to get the door of his cage unlatched." She smiled down at the bird and gave him a scratch on his head. Then she looked back up at the boys and narrowed her eyes. "What are you two doing here?"

Johnny walked to Peoni and clutched her by both shoulders. Looking very seriously into her eyes, he said, "Peoni, you are a nice person, and I'll miss your pointy hair."

"We've been called to FangSwan's office," interjected Joey.

Peoni's eyes went big and wet. It was a look she normally reserved for wounded squirrels or bent-winged pigeons. "Oh . . . boys, I'm so sorry." She hugged them both. "I . . . I always thought I'd know what to say."

"Well, you didn't have Renbow's class," said Joey. "We are *well* prepared."

"Do you want me to come with you? Maybe I could say something to FangSwan?"

That was easily the bravest thing anyone had ever offered to do for Joey. He felt an unwelcome swell of emotion in his chest. It was okay for a ninja to cry only if they were cradling the gasping body of a dying loved one. Even then it was required that they be sitting in a field of gently falling lotus blossoms. So Joey held his composure. "It's okay, Peoni. We got this."

WISEMAN NOTE: Before a particularly emotional battle some ninjas carry a sack of fresh-picked blossoms just in case they see any of their comrades starting to tear up.

"Let's have lunch tomorrow, Peoni! I'll buy us squid balls!" said Johnny, waving cheerfully. Johnny had gone to the happy place in his head, and neither Joey nor Peoni had the heart to call him back.

"Um . . . okay, Johnny, that would be"—*choke*—"nice . . ."

Joey and Johnny turned and continued down the last hallway before the staircase. Peoni watched them go, and in her mind they were walking through a field of gently falling lotus blossoms.

The Hall of Accusation was another charming idea from the depths of FangSwan's twisted mind. It was lovingly crafted by ninja artisans, many of whom forever gave up the arts after encountering the increasingly insane demands of the headmaster. It featured seventy-three statues of the most famously bloodthirsty ninja

masters, all striking increasingly judgmental poses. The first few merely stared down with their arms crossed like angry dads, but the farther down the hall you walked the meaner their eyes grew and the closer their pointing fingers came to your undeserving head.

It wasn't until Joey was nearly poked in the eye by the last ninja master's finger that he realized they had come to FangSwan's door. It was an imposing thing made of dark wood that featured an enormous swan with a single tooth poking from its beak. You could almost see a faint outline of the last student who had exited. Joey sighed. "I thought I was gonna go down dispatching a thousand enemies, maybe with something exploding in slow motion behind me."

"I thought there'd be bagpipes," said Johnny. "And my last act would be silencing them."

With a ponderous creak and a series of loud clunks, the door split at the wings of the swan and opened.

"Well, Johnny, I just hope there isn't a pee incident."

"Oh, did you mean . . ."

"No, Johnny. No, I didn't."

IN THE DEN
OF FANGSWAN

In which the boys HAVE made it to
Chapter 2, so they should be nothing
but thankful for the extra time.

"**M**aster FangSwan—Headmaster of Kick Foot Academy, Chieftain of the Twenty Screaming Winds, Lord of the Volcanic Lair of Blight, Slayer of the Ghost Samurai Horratto, and Vanquisher of the Beast Who Ate Mount Kimchi—will see you now." Vice Principal Zato ushered them in. His presence lightened Joey's mood somewhat. FangSwan would most likely not kill them with a witness present. But Zato was blind, so maybe he didn't count.

FangSwan, headmaster and founder of Kick Foot Academy, was a small man, and old. While some grow feeble or crumble with age, FangSwan seemed only to grow harder and sharper. Like an unexploded bomb, time had not made him any less dangerous, just increasingly unstable.

FangSwan would have looked good atop a throne of human skulls. In fact, really he looked out of place *not* sitting on one. The desk in front of him was a tree slab that seemed as though it had been beaten into a vague desk shape by bare hands. Like everything else in FangSwan's office, it appeared to have been defeated before it got there. Even his "Best Headmaster in the WORLD" mug looked as though it was being punished for betrayal.

FangSwan's hand poked from the sleeve of his long white robe. Joey just concentrated on the hand and tried to convince himself that it wasn't attached to this engine of destruction and sarcasm. The hand was the only part of the headmaster that Joey had enough courage to look at, and even that was an act of bravery. There wasn't a ninja alive who could tell you what color FangSwan's eyes were, and the not-alive ones were keeping quiet on the subject.

"Headmaster," Zato said. "Your students, Joey and Johnny." He could have added "the ninjas," but that would've been redundant in a ninja academy.

"Good morning, students," said a voice issuing from a few feet above the hand.

Ah, he was starting with "Good morning"—that was a really bad sign. It meant that he would be toying with them for a while.

Might as well have a mystery solved, thought Joey. With a grunt of effort he jerked his head up to look directly into Headmaster FangSwan's eyes. They were a nice shade of green.

Well, that's something, thought Joey. Not having time for a rewrite, Joey launched directly into his B-minus last-words speech. As Sensei Renbow had taught them, when facing imminent death, time was of the essence.

From behind Joey, Johnny called out, "Um, I like pancakes?"

The ancient headmaster silenced them with a look. His eyes flickered from one boy to another and rested a moment on the bouncing ball at the end of Johnny's antenna.

"What are Hoey and Dingle-Bopper babbling about, Vice Principal Zato?" said FangSwan in a voice that sounded like a sword being slowly pulled from its scabbard.

"Ah, I believe young student Joey is reciting his famous last words, part of Master Renbow's course work. Your other student, Johnny, is perhaps requesting a last meal," Zato said. He was standing behind FangSwan as he spoke. Was there a tiny hint of a smile at the corners of his lips? "They obviously believe you are going to kill them, Headmaster."

"Do you?" FangSwan asked, staring at Joey and Johnny. He slowly turned his head to one side. His neck made a small pop as it twisted. "Excellent." The word sounded cold, distant, and satisfied. "Not by my hand. Not today. You are here for another reason."

"If it's about the panda," Johnny said quickly, "I was only trying to help. I thought that they were supposed to be all black."

"It is not about the panda," FangSwan said through clenched teeth.

"I didn't know that ducks were . . ." Joey trailed off under the headmaster's steady gaze.

"Oh, I'm sorry, are you done talking?" FangSwan smiled. "Is it my turn to talk *in my own office?!*"

"Yes, sir! Sorry, sir!" Joey and Johnny yelped in unison.

"Hoey and Dingle-Bopper, I have no interest in any of your ramblings. I have a mission for the two of you." He turned back to Zato. "Incidentally, have pancakes removed from the breakfast menu."

Joey took his first breath since they had walked into the office. "A . . . a mission, Headmaster FangSwan?"

"Pancakes are *out*?" cried Johnny.

Zato interceded smoothly. "Master FangSwan, no doubt Joey and Johnny are deeply appreciative of the honor you have placed upon them. Their excitement has made them temporarily forget their place. I am sure they are ready to listen with rapt attention."

"Yes!" said Joey. "Everything he said!"

FangSwan's eyebrows grew marginally less violent. The amount of violence contained in his eyebrows could fuel several wars for many centuries. Even a tiny change in their character could be a life-altering detail all KFA students had learned to notice.

"We have an exchange student joining our school. They say that it's some foolish notion of cultivating community and sharing our knowledge, but I believe *he is a spy.* The two of you will mind him, and by mind him I mean *watch everything that he does and not leave*

him alone for a second!" The eyebrow-violence meter went up a notch.

"Does this include bathroom time?" asked Johnny. Joey winced.

"*Especially bathroom time!* Spies do their most important work during bathroom time," said Fang-Swan, twisting his hands into claws.

"Ugh!" said Johnny, looking uncomfortable. "What kind of information are these spies after?!"

I AM HUNGRY.

WHAT IS FOR DINNER?

LOOK, IT IS AN ADORABLE PUPPY.

Vice Principal Zato might have been blind, but he saw an opportunity to help the boys. He chose this moment to step out from behind the headmaster's chair. He had not been hiding, but the vice principal had a way of being unnoticed until he wished otherwise.

It was one of the many skills that had won Zato's membership in FangSwan's inner circle. An inner circle of which he is, and has ever been, the only member.

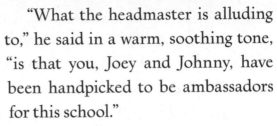

"What the headmaster is alluding to," he said in a warm, soothing tone, "is that you, Joey and Johnny, have been handpicked to be ambassadors for this school."

"Yes," FangSwan added, "I chose you so that the spy understands *exactly* how high a regard I have for him."

"It's a big job, boys, with a lot of responsibility, and a chance to make new friends. For all of us. Remember, you will be standing in for the headmaster and representing the whole school," Zato said.

FangSwan disagreed. "'Stand in'? No! No one can 'stand in' for me. When I am gone there will be a FangSwan-shaped hole in the universe. But fine. You're my handpicked 'ambassadors.' Just don't screw this up. Zato, show them the door."

The swan door shut behind them with a deep boom. To the boys' knowledge, it was the first time a student had left through that door without an immediate call for door repairs. The door had been damaged so many times that, in an effort to be helpful, the repairmen tried to reinforce it. This just had the unfortunate side effect of making students' exits more painful.

Joey looked down at his undamaged, unbroken body. He put a hand on his unsplintered ribs and touched a finger to each tooth still clinging to his gums.

Johnny was busily staring cross-eyed at the stone finger of ninja-master Shreddo Missaggi. Shreddo was famous for bragging that he could punch a finger through the moon. It was true, he did do it—but the jump left him too exhausted to get his finger unstuck afterward. Lack of oxygen took care of the rest. Shreddo had won his bet, but, man—he was dumb as a brick.

Directly opposite Shreddo was the ninja Twinkly-Puff. Before you snort, please understand that he stood at the very top of the pyramid of scary ninjas. He named himself Twinkly-Puff in the hope that it would lead to more opportunities for fights. It worked brilliantly. Not only did he score a major brawl everywhere he went, but thousands of proud warriors had to admit that they had been beaten by a man named Twinkly-Puff. Sadly, this strategy led to many young ninja copycats. There were a few years during the 1800s when you couldn't spit without hitting a ninja named Pudding-Mittens or Cuddle-Pumpkin. Luckily the problem solved itself when the Tiddly-Pomply-Pom clan went to war with the Black-Razor Storm clan. The staggeringly one-sided outcome of that war determined that cool names were back in fashion.

"Johnny! We aren't dead!"

"Ugh!" said Johnny. "I was kinda getting used to the idea of not having to write a to-do list for tomorrow."

"Well, item one on that list is: appreciate being alive!" Joey's stomach made an audible gurgle. "I'm hungry. I . . . I think I want to go to lunch."

"You want to go to *lunch*? But doesn't that mean ignoring item one on the to-do list?"

Ah, lunchtime! Such a delightful part of the day! You get a ham sandwich or some octopus, maybe a juice box and a flattened, plastic fruit thing. Most of the time it comes in a big happy box that has popular characters on it. (Ninjas would look really good on a lunchbox, I bet!) Lunchtime is like having Christmas in the middle of every day.

Of course, you think that only because you don't go to school at KFA. There was a brief time when lunch was pretty fun there too. The students used to get little bento-box lunches, which were so cute you'd just want to name them and keep them as pets. But that time was short-lived. Of the reported 273,000 attempts to assassinate FangSwan, only three came anywhere close to succeeding. And yes, one happened during lunchtime. So FangSwan decided that his students needed to be at their very highest state of alert during meals.

Joey and Johnny stood outside the cafeteria door, taking a brief moment to meditate and steel themselves. "You ready?"

Johnny took a deep breath. "Do it, Joey. Open the door!"

A chicken hurtled past their heads as they pulled the door handle. It buried itself deep into the stone wall behind them. "Oh! Chicken and dumplings!" cried Johnny cheerily.

They each snatched a plate out of the air and whipped out their chopsticks from hidden pockets. Students were doing backflips and cartwheels through a room thick with flying egg rolls, bowls of dipping sauces, and chickens with the occasional bite taken out of them. There were a few different styles of eating. A less skilled student might simply duck a head in and hope that something edible smacked him in the face. There were plenty who walked away with nothing but a mouthful of napkin and a saltshaker for lunch. Joey and Johnny bobbed and weaved their way through the food storm, finding the table where Peoni and Ting sat across from each other. Peoni stopped, wide-eyed, a bite of broccoli halfway to her mouth.

"You're not dead or broken!" she cried. She wanted to hug them, but it wasn't worth the loss of concentration.

Ting couldn't form words. He gripped a lunch tray in front of his face, allowing it to bear the brunt of the food onslaught. If something tasty dripped down his sleeve he'd risk taking a quick lick. All Ting's meals were sucked from his clothing. It explained why he constantly smelled of meatballs. "Jo . . . Jah! Nuh! Alive! Guh!" he said over the *spak, spak, spak* of pelting tidbits. Ting was a favorite target of the lunch ladies, but it wasn't really clear whether it was because they disliked him or because they felt the poor boy needed some meat on his bones.

Joey held up his chopsticks and pulled a chicken leg out of the meal-storm. "We're not just alive, Peoni, we've got a *mission!*"

"A mission from Fang-Swan?" she said, her smile quickly disappearing. "So you *are* going to die."

"Gah!" said Joey. "Why does everybody think we're going to die?"

"Well, did you read

the chapter heading?" said Peoni.

"It isn't even that dangerous! We just have to pick up an exchange student and watch him."

"So you're babysitting?" said Peoni, jerking her head to the side to avoid a muffin.

"You got that right," said Johnny, skewering a dumpling and giving it a quick dip in a passing bowl of sweet-and-sour sauce. "We even have to go to the bathroom with him."

"Oh, so it's worse—you two are on diaper duty!"

The shine was quickly wearing off

Joey and Johnny's precious mission. Joey snatched a green bean and chewed it as if he wanted it to suffer. Ting had a bit of good luck—a decent amount of gravy had soaked his forearm and he was making repulsive sucking sounds. Peoni moved her chair a little farther away, narrowly avoiding a multilevel cake complete with candles.

"Oh, look! It's FuShoe's birthday," cried Johnny, watching the lovely cake fly through the air.

FuShoe whipped her sai through the center of the cake, laughing as each half obliterated the two boys standing on either side of her. She was a brash girl who had the reputation of forcing her beaten opponents to smell her feet. There wasn't a boy at the school who didn't know what defeat smelled like.

"Remember when it was Brad's birthday and he sliced the cake into exactly the right number of pieces *and* got a piece in everyone's mouth?" said Johnny.

Ting certainly remembered. It was the first thing

he had ever eaten that didn't have lint on it.

"Can we please not mention Brad while I'm eating?" said Joey.

Brad was arguably the great-est student Kick Foot Academy had ever seen. He'd broken every record, making the phrase "Brad has broken a record!" sound like a broken record. Even FangSwan treated him with something that looked suspiciously like respect. But what really disgusted Joey was that even when Brad completely kicked your butt at something, he'd somehow manage to make  you look good *while* he was wiping the floor with you. So there was no way to hate the guy! Joey hated him for that.

"Joey," said Peoni, trying to distract him, "you don't suppose the exchange student is from Red Moon Clan, do you?"

Joey took a bean pod to the ear in surprise. "Peoni! I didn't even think of that! What if it's a Moony?"

Red Moon Clan was a rival to KFA in the same way that a guy who sells roasted rats in an alleyway could be called a rival to the five-star restaurant that stands across the street. They were an annoyance, not a threat. Gaining entrance into KFA was a grueling process involving days of pain and fear. To get into Red Moon Clan you needed to pay twenty-five dollars and draw a picture of Flippy the Ninja.

So it was a great surprise when Ting blurted out his first complete sentence of the lunch period: "Iwasthinkingoftransferringtothe RedMoonSchool!"

Peoni sliced away a cantaloupe that might have squashed Ting's head. "*Ting!* You can't be serious! You want to be a Moony?"

"I've been practicing drawing Flippy the Ninja!"

Ting said. "Other than the arms, I think it's pretty good." He showed off a drawing that looked like the gruesome aftermath of an accident involving some gum and spaghetti.

"Oh, I've drawn Flippy eight hundred times—you can totally have one of mine, Ting," said Johnny, pulling out a handful of crumpled drawings. "Here, here's one of Flippy riding a dinosaur, here's one of Flippy bowling with a caveman, here's Flippy speaking in Congress . . ."

"Johnny! Please tell me you haven't thought of joining Red Moon Clan too!" cried Peoni.

"Oh no," said Johnny, wiping a gravy stain from his drawing. "I just like drawing Flippy and his hilarious square head!"

"So when are you boys getting your new baby?" asked Peoni.

"Seven spiky samurai, Johnny!" said Joey, smacking his own head. "We never asked FangSwan which gondola the exchange student was coming in on!"

Johnny got up and started heading toward the door. "No problem. I'll just go ask him."

"Arrgh! No!" cried Joey, grabbing Johnny and hauling him back. "Remember what Master Renbow said: 'If the lion forgets to eat you, don't go back to thank him!'"

The four ninjas caught sight of Vice Principal Zato entering the cafeteria. The blind swordmaster drifted through the chaos calmly. He didn't appear to be trying to dodge anything, and yet not so much as a stray pickle touched him. The sight was so mesmerizing that by the time Zato reached them, the kids had forgotten to move and were getting pelted by the salad course.

"Students," said Zato, pulling a lettuce leaf from Peoni's brow, "I see you are getting a jump on your stealth homework. I truly thought you were the salad bar."

Ting was doing his best to remain unnoticed. There was no telling what the vice principal had overheard. Zato's ears were said to be so sharp that he got his daily news by standing on the mountain and listening to chatter from the city below.

"Ting," said Zato sharply, "I would like a word with you." He swept the pile of food from the boy and pulled him to his feet. As he led Ting from the room he called back over his shoulder, "Oh, boys, I suggest you leave for your mission after your last class tomorrow, and be sure to make haste. As Sensei Renbow says, 'The last gazelle is the first to catch the lion's eye.'"

WELCOME TO KFA

In which we learn that you might go to ninja school on a bus, but you leave in an ambulance.

It wasn't until lunch the next day that the four friends met up again. That day's fare was deli sandwiches, so the worst thing you had to look out for was a tub of mayo, or one of those green olives on a toothpick sword. It was a relatively calm day in the cafeteria, but that meant that the lunch ladies were saving up for something big. Soup day, or the even deadlier possibility: fondue. The hoses of boiling oil and cheese, the uncooked meat products, and alternatively sticky and slippery floors spelled danger for any ninja.

"We've only got two classes left and then it's off to get the spy," Joey said. He palmed a slice of bread and then wove his arm through the whirling cloud of paper-thin lunch meats and stacked himself a sandwich. He topped it off with two pickles and a kaiser roll. It was a huge sandwich, and Joey kindly split it with Ting.

"Don't prejudge. He, *or she*, might be nice," Peoni said. She had caught a bowl of macaroni salad and took a few bites with her chopsticks. "Oooh, it's good today."

"Maybe, but FangSwan said—" Joey began, but Peoni interrupted him.

"Oh, FangSwan, FangSwan. What if he told you to jump off a cliff? You wouldn't, would you?"

"Definitely," Joey said.

"Not a question," Ting offered. "The alternative is so much worse."

Peoni scoffed. "Where's Johnny? Johnny's with me."

Johnny had been whisking around the cafeteria chasing after olive swords. When he finally returned he had an oversize olive on each finger. Red and green plastic blades stuck through, looking like claws. He wiggled his fingers in Ting's face, saying, "Monster hands, Ting! I have monster hands!"

"No, Johnny!" said Ting, closing his eyes and slapping at Johnny's hand. "No monster hands! You'll give me nightmares!"

One of the thick-armed, gray-skinned lunch ladies

saw Johnny. She gave a gravelly laugh and hit him with a bag of chips.

"On that note," Joey said, "let's go to class."

Meditation

Sensei Ohm slid through the westernmost wall of the classroom, evoking a gasp from the class, and a full-blown spit take from Ting, who had just taken a sip from his water bottle. Have you ever seen a fully masked ninja do a spit take? It is a thing of beauty that normally requires them to go get a fresh mask from their locker.

"May I get a towel, Sensei Ohm?" Ting asked, raising one hand and wiping his face with the other.

"Certainly, dear, but do try to hurry," Ohm said. Her voice was pleasant and feminine, but that was the only indicator that Ohm was indeed a female . . . or human . . . or even belonged to the animal kingdom.

Sensei Ohm was a sphere of pure energy. Years ago she reached such an enlightened state that she no longer had need for her body, except for special occasions. Johnny heard that she kept it somewhere in Minnesota and returned once a month to clean, bathe, and feed it. Occasionally she took it out to attend a wedding or funeral.

At Kick Foot Academy, Ohm normally appeared as a ball of light approximately two feet in diameter. She was very easy on the eyes, producing a low-wattage glow in soft white with just a touch of cherry-blossom pink.

If desired, Ohm could generate a wide range of colors and intensities, or even full-blown three-dimensional projections. And there was that one time she single-handedly provided all the fireworks for the New Year's Eve party.

"Today we'll be delving into the meditation techniques used by Subterranean Mole Monks of Manchuria."

She hovered to the front of the classroom. Immediately Manchurian symbols, various woodcuts, and paintings were projected on the otherwise-blank walls. The pictures changed to match where Ohm was in her lesson plan. Some of them even displayed basic animations to better illustrate the movements she was describing.

Johnny's brain slowly filled with the knowledge on how to empty it again. He sat two chairs away from Joey, with Peoni in between them. Casually Johnny leaned back and made eye contact with Peoni, who smiled his way. In the corner of her notebook she had been doodling a squirrel. Making eye contact with Joey was also attempted, but experience told Johnny that nothing would come of it. Joey kept his eyes front with an insistent intensity that couldn't be healthy.

Eventually the class broke into smaller groups to practice their choice of the techniques discussed. Johnny joined up with Peoni, Ting, and Joey. They all agreed to Joey's suggestion of trying the Path of the Wrathful Badger.

It was the rather obscure practice of focusing one's anger into quick, enlightened motions in order to attain wisdom. Joey had been drawn to this method because it involved hitting people and required absolutely no chanting.

Less than a minute later the four friends stood in a square slapping one another in the face over and over. Wisely, they decided to alternate slapping partners. With Ting's weak, noodly arms every third blow felt like a vacation. Sadly, there was no such respite for Ting.

SLAP! SLAP! SLAP!

"OW!" cried Ting. "Peoni, quit hitting like a girl!

Try to hit like something much softer and weaker." He held a hand up to the side of his face. "I swear I can feel something wiggling around in there."

Slap. SLAP! SLAP!

"Yeah, your tongue," Joey said. "Less talking. More slapping!"

SLAP! Slap. SLAP!

"Good one," Peoni said. "I tasted blood that time."

The boys used to have strong feelings against hitting a girl, but those thoughts were simply impractical at a diversified ninja school like KFA. They quickly learned that if they didn't fight back, Peoni could and would rabbit-punch them into the hospital.

SLAP! SLAP! Slap. On the other hand, it was particularly amusing to slap Johnny in the face. Every hit made his dooley-bopper spin as if you were doing a trick with a yo-yo.

"So the goal is to get mad?" Johnny asked, his words a little muffled from his swollen cheeks.

"Yes," said Joey through gritted teeth.

SLAP! SLAP! SLAP! That round made Ting take a knee.

"And this leads to enlightenment?" Johnny asked.

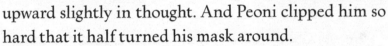

"Yes!" Joey repeated.

"How?"

Slap. SLAP! SLAP!

Joey's face angled upward slightly in thought. And Peoni clipped him so hard that it half turned his mask around.

"Ow!" he said, trying to twist his mask back into place. "I—I don't know."

SLAP! Slap. SLAP!

"Enlightenment better come soon," Peoni said. "I got less of a beating in fight class today, and Kendu made us climb into a sleeping bag with a snapping turtle."

SLAP! SLAP! Slap.

"All at once, or one at a time?" Johnny asked.

"One at a time," Peoni said. "How would the whole class fit in a sleeping bag?"

"Could've been a big sleeping bag."

SLAP! SLAP! SLAP!

"Okay, okay. Stop!" Ting called out. "I have found enlightenment! New knowledge has been given to me."

"Really?" Joey asked. "What knowledge?"

"I *know* I want you people to stop hitting me in the face."

The rest nodded in silent agreement. Ting shed a few tears of gratitude, and then he had himself a little cry. Johnny got a round of ice packs from the nurse and the foursome collapsed into their chairs.

Sensei Ohm spoke. "Class, quiet. I want everyone's attention here."

Ohm generated a small spotlight focused on a lone student. He looked a little embarrassed to be singled out but then smiled and focused on his task. A low chanting came in perfect rhythm from his mouth as his hands pressed thumb into middle finger. Palms up, his hands slowly rose until they were nearly chest high—and then it happened.

His eyes rolled back in his head and his neck arched. A pleasing glow spread outward from under his skin as his body lifted a foot from the ground. Now the rich sound of his baritone chanting didn't just fill the room; it filled the other students' minds. The event lasted only moments, and then as quickly as it came, it was gone.

"Bradley has achieved enlightenment, children.

Isn't that wonderful?" Sensei Ohm beamed . . . literally.

"I can only hold it for a couple of seconds," he said humbly. "The universe is just so vast."

"Man, he's a good ninja," Johnny said. "He achieved enlightenment in thirty-seven minutes. His way sure beats face-slapping."

"Brad . . . ," Joey growled under his breath, and then the bell rang.

Fight Class

Fight class was normally Joey and Johnny's favorite. Always lively and dangerous, and always, always unexpected—even today, when they had Peoni's forewarning about the turtle and the sleeping bag. They certainly could not have guessed how big the turtle was, or that it had two heads.

All ninjas remember their first fight class. Joey and Johnny certainly remembered theirs, just a year earlier. The boys had hesitantly walked into a large, roughly round classroom with a high-raftered ceiling. Crates, trunks, and boxes of all sorts were precariously stacked along the walls. Shafts of soft light seeped in from high, square windows illuminating dust motes like tiny fireflies.

In the middle of the room was a huge pile of the fluffiest pillows Joey or Johnny had ever seen. The kind of pillows that could make clouds jealous. They were loosely contained in mismatched pillowcases.

Their teacher entered the room with a flutter of wings. Sensei Kendu was a Tengu, a race of fierce, birdlike demons that legend states taught the very first ninjas how to use their swords. It was told in whispers among the students that she taught at KFA because FangSwan had beaten her in a fair duel.

She was a little shorter than a typical human woman, with a beaked face and beautiful golden eyes. Her arms were a blend of human and bird, ending in hands that were capable of wielding any human weapon, but that could also pull her into the air like an eagle.

Johnny felt that her most noteworthy feature was the long curtain of raven-black hair that she kept perfectly groomed. At different times it appeared to be a cloak, a wave, or a whip, depending on how Kendu used it.

Joey's focus was on her taloned toes, but that's just because bird feet freaked him out.

Sensei Kendu walked past the young ninjas gathered before her. Some bowed their heads, others met her gaze, while a few took nervous steps backward. She gestured toward the pillows.

"Fight," she said. It was a human voice. No, that's not quite right, it was the talented mimicry of a human voice. Like the speech of an African gray parrot.

No one moved. Sensei Kendu hopped and flipped over the fluffy pile. She gestured at them again, this time with both arms.

"Fight." The word was still calm but harder now.

Students slowly spread out around the pillows. Braver souls picked one up, or passed one over to their friends.

"Fight." The tone now insistent.

Finally a ninja turned and halfheartedly hit

another with one of the larger pillows. The victim let out a little nervous laugh and then, seeing that no reprimand was coming, turned to his attacker and responded in kind.

Sensei Kendu seemed to smile. *"Fight!"* she said again, but now it was both joyous and infectious. A cheer rose from the ninjas as a melee ensued. The next forty-five minutes was some of the most fun Joey and Johnny could remember having at KFA. Pillows flew like plushy shuriken. The students leapt and turned and hit one another with feather-bursting force. Seemingly everyone and everything was a target. It didn't even matter if you lost your pillow; there were plenty more for the taking. The air filled with falling feathers, squealing students, and the clucking laughter of Sensei Kendu.

When she finally said "Stop," there was an audible groan of disappointment.

The next session, eager students burst into class to find the room restored to its previous arrangement. Only now, in the middle of the floor, instead of pillows there was a large pile of pipe wrenches.

There was a flutter behind them and the doors swung shut.

Sensei Kendu smiled her strange bird smile and said, "Fight."

A WALK IN THE WOODS

In which we reveal that this is just a
book about nature walks and we put
ninjas on the cover to sell it. HA!

Kick Foot Academy was carved into the face of one of the many mountains surrounding the city of Lemming Falls. Snuggled deep in a nest of craggy hilltops and tree plumage, the city was so sheltered from the rest of the world that if the planet were to blow up, Lemming Falls would most likely continue on, blissfully unaware. Blissful, that is, until chunks of neighboring states started obscuring its view of the moon.

You might be picturing a Podunk village with three cows and a gas station, but it had plenty of skyscrapers and all sorts of other sticky-outty buildings bristling from its foundations. Seclusion had led Lemming Falls to be unlike anywhere else in the country. On any given day citizens had come to accept, perhaps even to expect, that the rush-hour traffic was likely to be caused by a superhero battle or giant squid attack. You were still late to work, but it was certainly more interesting than a fender bender on 490.

The city also had Lemming's Leap, a cliff that towered over the buildings and cut the city into two neat halves. Lemming's Leap was world famous as the premier destination for suicidal rodents. Once a year an uncountable number of lemmings would run straight up the cliff's ridge and hurl their little bodies off the top, raining down on the city below. Since the phrase "You might get hit on the head with a lemming" reads poorly in a tour guide, the city's mayor organized "the Lemming Drop Festival." With help from the superhero community, each and every misguided animal would get rescued in a grand televised celebration. The tourists flocked to the festival by the thousands and everyone bought a T-shirt.

As the city grew and spread into the surrounding mountains, its good citizens needed more than just the usual array of buses and trains to get around. So a complex gondola system was put in place. Looking like sleek bubbles made of metal and glass, the gondolas hung from hooks connected to a vast web of thick steel cables. These cables could haul people up into the highest peaks or drag them down into the depths of the city's underwater shopping mall. In fact the only place the gondola couldn't take you was the Kick Foot Academy. The name FangSwan had started wars and stopped hearts. That same name had been whispered into the ear of one Susan Softwater, chair of the gondola zoning committee, and a moment later KFA's mountain was listed as a forest preserve.

WISEMAN NOTE: Incidentally, a small group of monks known as the Lovers of the Lovely Word make their home in one of the caves close to my mountain peak. They find the English language so important that each month they choose a different word to chant continuously. The word for September was "gondola." It works beautifully: gondola . . . gondola . . . gondola . . . see? Unfortunately the word for October was "Scranton." It inspired me to buy noise-canceling headphones.

To get to the closest gondola station Joey and Johnny had a four-hour trek across treacherous territory that held all manner of dangerous beasts, herbs, and fungi. Still, it wasn't enough to keep Joey interested in the journey.

"This is definitely not ninja," Joey griped.

"A quest through

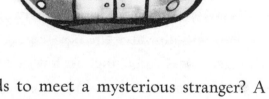

uncharted woods to meet a mysterious stranger? A spy?" Johnny asked. "Sounds pretty ninja to me."

"Not that. This." Joey gestured to the calm, pastoral trees around them. A leaf broke free as he looked up and flipped in charmingly lazy loops to the ground. "This is literally a walk in the park."

Joey was falling for one of nature's greatest tricks. It's beautiful. It's so beautiful and peaceful-seeming that we forget that it can be cold and cruel. I'd like to point out that not a stone's throw away, a razor-backed black bear was in a life-and-death struggle with a plant that was part ivy, part Venus flytrap, and all thorns. The boys would've heard its growls if the bear hadn't had its mouth full of ropey vines. So enjoy your "walk in the park," because it's just one wolf pack away from being a "run for your life."

Now go outside and play, kids.

"We should be swinging on grappling hooks, or sprinting blindfolded between the trees," said Joey.

"We could do cartwheels," Johnny offered.

"Not until thirty minutes after lunch."

They wandered a bit farther, when Johnny brightened up. Recognizing the territory, he suggested, "How about a shortcut?"

"Call it a 'secret path' and you're on," declared Joey.

Ten minutes later the boys emerged from a thorny thicket into a clearing. A few huts were scattered around a communal cooking fire. They were the ramshackle kind of hut, made from things found in the forest: tree branches, mud, and coarsely woven grasses.

They were also huge! Built for people easily half again as tall as the tallest person you've ever known. Let's see, that's six foot seven divided by two and then added to itself . . . three point five converts to seven halves . . . combine that with seven multiplied by two equals twenty-one . . . Six and three and ten and a half . . . round up and you get . . . really, *really* big.

All around the boys—adjusting a crude leather bootstrap, sharpening a bone dagger, or crouched by the fire cooking something that is best not described in great detail—were Oni. Oni were not used to anything stumbling into their camp. There was an unspoken rule of the forest that such an action would end badly for said stumbler. Unspoken, but at the same time written in stone.

Joey and Johnny were not up on their reading.

Surprise was their momentary ally as all activity and sounds ceased and all heads turned to face the two small ninjas. Somehow even the crackling of the fire seemed subdued. There are many kinds of silence in the world, and this one was a pool of calm before a

crashing wave of noise. Noise mostly filled with people screaming, *"Ow!"*

"Johnny."

"Yes, Joey?"

"This is not a shortcut."

"It is now," said Johnny.

The animal-skin door flap covering the entrance of the central hut flipped back, revealing the largest Oni the boys had ever seen. In most ways the Oni chieftain was built like a human, only made with crude, oversize tools. It was somewhere over eleven feet tall and broad across the shoulders, belly, and hips. Muscular, blue-skinned arms, longer than those of a man, hung low. One of its hands, as large as a small barrel, wrapped around the handle of a massive wooden club studded

with chunks of raw iron and semiprecious stones. The legs were short like a gorilla's. Its snarling face was missing a tusk.

A look of recognition passed between Johnny and the creature. The Oni's eyes, a mix of bloodshot and yellow, narrowed with hatred. Joey muttered an ancient ninja curse under his breath.

"Hello again." Johnny waved. "How's the tooth?"

Just before the cool mountain air was split by a bellowing battle cry, Joey managed to scream, *"Run!"*

A tree exploded into splinters as the chieftain's kanabo hummed inches from Joey's chest. To his right another tree, this one thicker than his torso, turned into a fine spray of toothpicks. As long as they managed to keep going in the right direction, the boys were now making excellent time. Few things are so motivating as being chased down a mountain by an outraged clan of Oni.

Johnny had drawn his clown hammer from wherever it was that he kept it. It was disturbing to watch if you'd never seen him do it before. He'd just reach behind his back and suddenly it was in his hand. The hammer was four feet long and weighed over thirty-five pounds. Even the teachers at KFA avoided asking too many questions about where it went.

Dodging club and claw, Johnny ran straight up a tree trunk and used it to jump backward over a slavering assailant. He delivered a spine-shortening thump to his attacker's head that seemed to do little more than annoy it. Onis have been known to win head-butting contests with bronze statues.

Meanwhile Joey kept strictly to the defensive while trying to remember the right ninja lesson for this situation. As Sensei Renbow often said, "The best way of dealing with an enemy is with an open fist." And no, he didn't mean slap them.

The chieftain brought his kanabo crashing down, missing Joey so narrowly his clothes ruffled in the breeze. As the great club rose, Joey landed on its shaft. He balanced on the edge as it lifted until he was at eye level with the blue behemoth.

"Please accept our humble apologies for disturbing your village and taking your tooth," Joey said.

Sensei Renbow would have been proud of Joey's diplomacy, horrified by his timing. You send diplomats in before or after a battle, *not* during. Predictably, Joey's words only fed the fire of the Oni's rage.

"Additional apologies in advance for this," Joey said.

The chieftain's arms flexed as he tried to smear Joey against a tree like a pat of butter. Joey sprinted down the length of the swinging club and landed so many kicks to the chieftain's forehead that an onlooker might have thought he was attempting to Riverdance. The

Oni roared and fell backward, hurling his club into the air. Joey flipped out of the way, landing neatly on a tree branch. He watched as the flailing chieftain tripped into the fiery torch held by one of his enraged brothers. His filthy loincloth instantly went up in flames.

Since the Oni are featured so prominently in ninja theater, Sensei Renbow had prepared his students well regarding their social habits. For example, it is a traditional part of Oni culture to set fire to the groom on the day he is to be married. So you can imagine the confusion it caused among the rampaging tribe when it appeared that their chieftain was preparing for a surprise wedding. His fellows broke off their attack, scattering into the woods to gather flowers and presents. The chieftain howled off into the forest, a glowing beacon for his imaginary bride.

"Soooooo ninja!" Joey said to an impressed-looking squirrel.

BUMPING INTO THE MOON

In which the boys suffer a brutal mooning.
Close your eyes, kids.

Two bruised and tired ninjas limped into the gondola station forty-five minutes ahead of schedule, despite their journey being two miles longer than it had to be.

Joey slapped Johnny on the back. "Nice shortcut!"

"Thanks, but know the best part?" Johnny asked.

"What?"

"Now I've got a matched set!" Johnny held up the chieftain's other tusk.

The gondola station was a place of waiting. Like many such places, it was not designed to be comfortable. Make a waiting room too comfortable and you might not want to leave. You'd be happy to sit in comfort and ignore your doctor's visit, or miss your train. A proper waiting room puts everyone in it in a slight state of agitation, thus enhancing your enjoyment when you finally get to leave.

The boys found a hard metal bench and slumped onto it. Looking up, they were faced with the giant cheerful eyes of Flippy the Ninja peeking at them from over the top of the gondola station.

The billboard was black, white, and red. Flippy waved his simplified hand at passersby. A huge word balloon was painted behind him, proudly declaring, *"Flippy says, You can be a NINJA!"* The Red Moon logo was plastered up there too. The sign was well designed and obviously effective, but there was nothing ninja about any of it.

Nor was there anything ninja about the Moonies themselves. Recently a graduate of Red Moon Clan had come to Kick Foot Academy. He boldly declared that he had learned all that Red Moon Clan could teach and wished to continue his training. He also claimed his name was Dragon Stormfist, which got a chuckle.

FangSwan had refused to acknowledge the man was even in the room. Instead he cruelly pretended to be distracted by a bothersome gnat anytime "Dragon" spoke. Eventually Zato arranged some light sparring with Ting to test the man's abilities. Five minutes later Dragon Stormfist left . . . crying. He never came back. Remember, this was Ting he was fighting. *Ting!*

On the bright side, Ting still talks about it as his "best day ever."

The squeak of the gondola grabbed the boys' attention and they quickly tried to smarten themselves up to greet their "guest," spy or not. They still had their pride.

Not many people came to KFA. Students, merchants bringing the occasional supplies, and once in a great while an assassin or rogue samurai might travel up the mountain . . . but they rarely took the gondola.

A couple of passengers walked onto the platform, cast an odd look at the two ninjas standing at attention, and then went about their business. Joey and

Johnny stood their ground and waited. And waited. And waited. The doors eventually shut and the gondola circled, heading back down the mountain.

"Huh," said Johnny.

"We're obviously earlier than we thought. He'll be on the next one," Joey said.

He wasn't on the next one, or the one after that. Eventually it started getting cold and the boys sat on the uncomfortable bench, huddling together for warmth. After the gondola came and went a fourth time without delivering the exchange student, Joey and Johnny stopped rising off the bench. Sometime after the seventh cycle the lights flickered and went off. The squeaking wheel that supported the cable came to a stop. The gondola had closed for the evening.

Sometime after that the boys fell asleep.

There was a sound in the night. A combination of a bombshell dropping and the distant wail of someone screaming as though their feet were on fire. It started small, but the sound grew and filled the mountainside.

Joey and Johnny leapt into the air as a flaming comet smashed into the Red Moon billboard, with a sign-shattering *FABOOM!*

"Whatthewhatwhat?" Joey said, pointing his katana in all directions at once.

"Flippy's on fire!" Johnny said.

It was true: the comet had hit right in the middle of Flippy's face and a ring of fire was spreading across the billboard. From somewhere behind the sign came a muffed "Ow."

On the other side of the billboard a figure lay motionless. His feet were on fire. Ah, that would

explain the scream.

The body wasn't moving, but the occasional groan was a definite indication of life. One of his legs was obviously broken, and he was dressed in the red shinobi fuku of a Red Moon trainee ("shinobi fuku" is just fancy talk for "ninja pajamas"). Heavy metal tubes that vaguely resembled moon boots were strapped to the ends of his legs, and . . . his feet were on fire. It's worth mentioning twice.

"This guy's a Moony," Joey said.

"I know," said Johnny, "and it looks like he's getting married too."

"Why here? Why now? What are Moonies doing so close to KFA? Did they abduct our exchange student? Is the exchange student a Moony spy and this is one of his contacts? What's going on here?"

"I don't know," said Johnny, "but maybe we should put his feet out!"

"Oh, sorry."

The boys quickly extinguished the flames, removed the blistering-hot metal boots, and surveyed the damage. Ninjas are used to seeing a lot of injuries. A younger ninja sees most of those injuries on his own body. So Joey and Johnny had a certain nurse-like expertise at assessing wounds of all sorts. Quickly, quietly, they splinted the leg and applied salve to the red, tender skin between foot and knee.

Before you ask, yes. A ninja always has a first-aid kit handy. Sure, the legends would rather talk of a katana that strikes like a lightning bolt, or a shadow cloak made of living ravens. But the quiet hero is the ninja's trusty first-aid kit. Raven bites can be nasty.

Joey said, "The leg's broken, but the burns could've been a lot worse."

Johnny was poking at the metal leg tubes, but they were still too hot to handle. There were buttons and dials at the top of each boot and large vents in the soles. One of which was dripping some kind of liquid.

Modern technology was not unknown to ninjas; they simply didn't use it. Joey and Johnny knew about airplanes, and computers, and reduced-water-flow toilets, but that's where it ended. The boots were obviously very advanced, so why was a ninja wearing them?

"Looks like we've got a mystery," Johnny said.

"No!" said a voice. "No mystery."

Behind them stood a small crowd of Red Moon ninjas. Some of them were panting heavily from their trek up the mountainside. Some had to sit down. A few had even pulled their face masks down to allow a better flow of oxygen. Only a handful held a martial-arts stance, but they were sloppy at it. And no two stances were alike, as if they were just copying something they had seen in a movie once.

The one who had spoken was dressed in black with a red disk upon his forehead. This identified him as a ninja-sergeant-master-of-the-west-winds, or something. The rest wore red novice robes.

"No mystery," he repeated.
"Just a camping accident."

"A what?" Joey asked.

"You heard me, just a little campfire accident. Nothing to be concerned about."

Joey looked at the still-burning hole in the Red Moon billboard. The fire had spread and one of the supporting posts was beginning to sag.

"Campfire accident . . . right," Joey said.

"It's really not any of your concern," the leader said. "So we'll just collect Rufus and go."

Joey eyed the group. With any luck it wouldn't come to a fight. He had counted sixteen Moonies, and it'd just be embarrassing to spar with fewer than twenty. Maybe if he could persuade Johnny to sit this one out . . .

"What are you doing so close to KFA, anyway?"

"No more questions!" the leader said with more confidence than Joey thought he deserved. "You are alone here, no FangSwan to come to your rescue."

"Don't say his name," whimpered a Moony in the back.

It only goes to show just how little they knew Fang-Swan. If he *had* been there, he'd probably have made Joey and Johnny wear blindfolds, or fight all the Moonies in alphabetical order.

"What's up with these boots?" Johnny asked.

"Larry, they know about the boots!" someone said nervously.

The leader, Larry, cringed a little at that. "We'll be taking those, too. And if you think you can stop us, just remember we have you outnumbered eight tooooooo— Ow. *Ow.* Okay. Okay. Okay. Justtakeiteasy. Take it easy."

Larry, being larger and older than either of the boys, had tried a little intimidation. It didn't work. The moment he tried to poke Joey in the chest, a snap-dragon wrist-lock immobilized Larry's arm up to the shoulder and sent him slowly sinking to his knees.

The rest of the Moonies gasped as one, and a series of soft electronic hums momentarily filled the night air. Little lights started flickering on various pieces of strange equipment worn by all the Red Moon Clan members.

"Watch out," one of them said. "They're *real* ninjas."

The Moonies' belts and sashes were loaded with big, bulky pockets and tiny LEDs. A heavyset boy put on a half-domed helmet. After it was hurriedly fastened, he pushed a button on the chin strap that started a small

diesel engine with no apparent purpose. A device that
looked like the offspring of a bazooka and a catapult
was leveled at Joey and Johnny from their right. The
smallest Moony was wearing what had to be a jet pack,
but he kept looking at Rufus's unconscious form and
sweating.

The nervous tension oozing from the Moonies was
almost thick enough to see.

"Wow, Joey," Johnny said, "look at the neat toys.
These guys look like action figures!"

"Definitely not ninja, though," Joey said.

"Says the guy with a dooley-bopper!"

"That's Johnny," Joey said. "I'm Joey!"

"Sorry," said the Moony who spoke earlier. "We're all wearing masks. Sometimes it's hard to tell who actually spoke."

"Fair enough," Joey said. "Okay, I'm going to let Larry up now. Let's all remain calm and work this out."

This was Joey's second try with diplomacy today. If it didn't work this time he was going to go back to punching trouble in the face. He moved slowly as he spoke, keeping his eyes on the various weapons and devices shakily aimed in their direction.

"Okay, Johnny and I haven't even drawn our weapons, so—"

"They have weapons!" someone squeaked from the back.

Chaos erupted. A few lights flashed and different-colored beams lanced up into the night sky. A Moony fired a large tube that made a *POOM!* sound and flung a net over some of his compatriots.

"No!" cried Larry as a big metal onion was hurled directly at his face.

He needn't have worried, because Johnny was there ninja-quick, swinging his clown hammer with perfect precision. The wooden head of the mallet connected with the metal vegetable and suddenly the world filled with tiny, angry bees.

The bees—actually poison-tipped darts—shot out in every direction. At the dead center of the blast Johnny had no chance of dodging them, and he fell as dozens sank into his skin. Joey avoided most of the darts, using Larry's meaty frame as a shield. Unfortunately a lucky shot slipped between the unconscious Moony's legs and sank into Joey's right foot.

Dropping Larry's slack body, Joey took a final glance around the gondola station. There wasn't a single surface that had not been pierced by the darts. Most of the windows had been broken, and the walls looked like a madman's dot-to-dot book.

Red Moon had fared no better—they had all dropped in undignified piles. That little kid must've activated his jet pack when he got knocked out, because he was spiraling away above the trees and down the mountain.

Things were getting hazy, but Joey was vaguely satisfied to be the last man standing. He tried to get out his famous last words—maybe a security camera would capture them on tape—but his lips refused to cooperate and Larry was starting to look like a big comfy pillow. A big comfy pillow studded with hundreds of tiny bees.

WISEMAN NOTE: The device that played such a pivotal role here is commonly called a Stunion. Basically it's a big metal ball that blooms like a flower when struck, at which point it releases a cloud of tiny stun darts. The effective range is about twenty feet or so, a fact that the Red Moons clearly forgot.

Hah! Look at that ball of knowledge I just lobbed at you. Try getting that from a goat-herding wiseman. Just you try.

Oh, and I owe an apology to Larry. He *did* need to worry.

INTO THE VOID

In which it really does look like
the boys are dead. Sorry, everyone,
bummer of an ending.

"Johnny?"

"Yes, Joey."

"I think we're dead."

"Really? I was told there'd be cake. Do you see any cake?"

"I don't see any anything."

Joey gestured to grand space around them. There was nothing, and nothing, and the distant twinkle of tiny lights that might have been stars. Admittedly, stars didn't normally move around like that, but it was noticeable only if you really looked for it.

"Oh, to be killed by Moonies! We've got to be the

worst ninjas ever," Joey said. "They're going to write it up in the scrolls as an example of how *not* to die."

"It isn't that bad."

"Johnny. We. Are. *Dead*. We've reached bad's farthest limit!"

"At least it wasn't just one of us."

Joey raised a finger to argue that a double death was definitely worse, but then he let his finger drop. Fearing that he was walking a sword's edge of sappiness, he said, "Yeah, okay, I'm glad you're here, Johnny."

"Me too, but I'd rather be alive, I think."

Joey floated over to Johnny's side. "Good. Then

here's the plan. When the Grim Reaper shows his face we beat him up until he tells us how to be alive again." He spoke the words quietly in case the void was listening.

"How?"

"He's a big skeleton in a robe, right?"

"Yes, he definitely is," Johnny said.

"And what are skeletons made of?"

"Bones." Johnny's eyes widened when he made the connection. "And we've been trained to break those since we first entered Kick Foot Academy."

"This guy is gonna be dust," said Joey, smacking his fist into his palm.

The upswing in their mood soured slightly when Joey reached over his shoulder to grab his katana and found it gone.

"Oh yeah," he said, "my sword is still on my body. It's not like you can take it with you."

"I can," Johnny said. The young ninja was experimentally swinging a silvery version of his clown hammer. A huge, helicopter-like twirl spun Johnny through space, leaving a subtle shimmering glow in the wake of the translucent mallet.

Joey grimaced. "I should've guessed the two of you were inseparable."

"I dub thee 'Skull Thumper,'" said Johnny, swishing a silvery comet tail over Joey's head. Finally, the two

boys sat
down side
by side in the
nothingness and
waited for death.

"I can't believe no
one else ever thought to
do this before," said Johnny.

Waiting comes naturally
to the dead, but not to Joey and
Johnny. So when they finally met
the Grim Reaper they were perhaps a
little too eager to fight for their lives.

The Reaper came floating through
the darkness, mumbling under his breath.
Instead of riding a spectral horse, he was sitting
in the lotus position. This might have seemed odd,
but in this space without ground or gravity a horse
would've just been problematic anyway.

His long, white, bony body had the same dull, silver
glow as Johnny's hammer. There were a few odd details
that might have stopped a more astute observer—no
robes, no scythe, and what was up with the beard? But

the Reaper was almost upon them and Joey knew they had to act.

"We're in luck, his eyes are closed," Joey said.

"Um, I don't think skulls have eyelids, Joey."

"Now, now. Get him now!" replied Joey.

Twin shadows rocketed through the inky black at the rapidly approaching Grim Reaper.

"Wha?!" was all he had time to say before being bounced between fist, foot, and glowing clown hammer. It was over before it started and the silver figure lay prone before them. As the last wisps of consciousness fled he heard the overzealous boy ninjas talking.

"Joey?"

"Yes, Johnny?"

"I don't think this is the Grim Reaper."

And *that's* how I met Joey and Johnny.

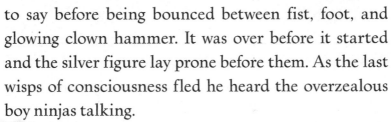

Time passed. Indistinct sounds mumbled by. Shadows shifted and movements were made. I wish I could say I awoke with a witty comeback, but I believe my first words were "Huzzit? What? How did you? Who?" My attackers were bending over me. There was nothing of them to see but eyes and eyebrows, but at least they held a look of concern.

"Oh," I said. "Ninjas."

"Yes, sir," they said.

"Great."

Joey was kneeling beside me and Johnny was doing his best to make his mallet look as nonthreatening as possible.

"We apologize *again* for sneaking up and attacking you," Joey said.

"'Again'?" I asked.

"We said it a lot right after you went down, but I don't think you heard us," Joey said.

Behind his mask his eyes were pleading and hopeful.

"And I'm soooo sorry I hit you with my clown hammer . . . twice," Johnny added.

Shrugging off Joey's helping hand, I stood as regally as I could. I threw in a little hand flourish but to no effect. Normally the old wiseman-mystic posturing wows the crowd, but it was hard to give an aloof stare with a rapidly swelling black eye.

"Sir," Johnny asked, "I know we just beat you up, but we were hoping that you could help us not be dead."

"Don't you know where you are?"

"No, sir," they said together. Polite little twits when they're not beating the pudding out of an old man.

"Then how did you get here?"

"We died, sir." The voices were so small and sad that I felt myself softening to their plight. Then I took a deep breath and my bruised rib sapped the empathy right out of me.

"No," I said, "you didn't."

Joey and Johnny were not dead. They had never been dead.

"Welcome to the astral plane," I said.

The astral plane is a place of mind and spirit and can be reached in different ways, including meditation. I had been on one of my daily astral constitutionals when the two confused ninjas started pounding the stuffing out of my astral body, a feat more impressive than it sounds since the astral plane is not a physical place. In this place I wasn't supposed to have a body, with or without stuffing.

Wisemen are always questing for new knowledge. Today I became the first person to learn that your astral form could be knocked out. See, there's a silver lining in everything if you look hard enough.

Yay.

"I take it," I said, trying to work a kink out of my astral back, "that this is your first time visiting."

"Yes, sir," they said.

Meditation had never been Joey or Johnny's strongest subject, as it rarely involved hitting something. If you asked what the word "transcendental" meant, Joey would tell you, "It involves having your teeth cleaned in the back of a moving truck."

It didn't.

It's not that Joey didn't try to meditate. He tried as hard as he possibly could, which, unfortunately, is the very opposite of letting go. He would sit cross-legged in class straining so hard to drift freely through the astral plane that sweat would trickle down his brow. Instead of becoming a spiritual traveler who was one with everything, he just looked like a boy who had eaten too much cheese.

Johnny was different. Funny, now that I think about it: it's hard to describe anything Johnny does without using the word "different." Unlike Joey, Johnny got quite high marks in his meditational studies. He just didn't understand how.

When Sensei Ohm asked Johnny the meaning of "transcendental," she got "A rare breed of singing fish?"

If Sensei Ohm had had a forehead to rub, she would've rubbed it.

Ohm couldn't exactly fault Johnny on this answer. In the astral plane, wanderers move with their life, mind, and experiences swirling around them like a song. Their every action in that realm holds a fluid grace not seen in the mortal plane. And a silver cord trails wavelike behind them keeping them tied to their physical body.

A singing fish.

It wasn't . . . wrong, but Sensei Ohm would think long and hard about whether the answer was blind luck, or brilliant poetry. It was like this with all Johnny's answers in her class. His high marks were partly due to those answers, and partly due to the undeniable fact that Johnny spent most of his life in a trancelike state.

He was obviously doing *something* right.

"We're in the astral plane?" Joey asked. "How?"

"Purple tiger mountain octopus toxin," I said.

"What?" said Joey.

There. That head-cocking look of uncomprehending bafflement is the whole reason I became a wiseman in the first place. The moment when you've blown someone's mind so thoroughly that they don't even know which way is up anymore. That's not just being the smartest guy in the room. That's being the smartest guy for a hundred miles in every direction. That's pure wisemanery.

"Are you just saying crazy stuff?" Johnny asked. "Because that's kind of my thing."

"Hmmph. As ninjas you've obviously had some training in meditation, but you're young and have never successfully crossed over. The connection to your physical body is just too strong. Too hard to let go of. Now, I'm guessing you both got hit by some kind of dart. The octo-toxin is both a neuron inhibitor and muscle relaxant.

"Speaking of that, I hope neither of you boys had to go to the bathroom when you got tagged."

Not letting them dwell on that upsetting image, I rolled on. Black eye or no black eye, I was in the swing of it now.

"You lost connection with your bodies, but your minds tried to fight on. Subconsciously tapping into your training, you both jumped ship into the astral plane. Where you found an innocent old man and reminded him that the world can be a dangerous place. Simple as that."

There was a span of silence, which I briefly basked in. Notice how I did not even once mention a goat or goat-related product.

"How do you know all that stuff?" Joey asked.

"Hmmph. How? HOW?! I am a wiseman. It so

happens that I'm *your* wiseman. It's my *job* to know things—"

Johnny leaned over to Joey's ear. "I don't remember getting a wiseman," he whispered. "When did you buy a wiseman?"

This was not an official consultation. There was no journey (a journey is a very important metaphor when learning new things), and generally a consultation does not begin with my clients giving me a severe beating. So, technically I wasn't required to tell them anything, but there was just so much for them to know. Big things were afoot, and these kids were going to need all the help they could get.

Decision made, I fluffed up my beard with one hand while pointing at my temple with mystic certainty with the other. I bugged out my eyes and let my gaze bore into the boys' skulls. I even flared out my astral aura so I appeared to be awash in pale silver flames. A simple trick, but these guys were noobs.

I spoke:

> *"You are not dead, shall soon awake*
> *But listen well, do not mistake*
> *A knight is close, and then goes far*
> *Trapped inside the up-down car*
> *Three challenges will come to thee*
> *The first a duel, the next—can't see*

The third a fight between two schools
To test his faith in honor and rules."

"Wow!" Joey said.

"I know," I said.

Johnny's head moved in small motions as he thought through the riddle. Soon his dooley-bopper was spinning in a tiny circle. He raised a hand hesitantly.

"I'm sorry, but I don't recognize the song those lyrics come from," Johnny said.

"Hmmph! They're not lyrics from a song," I said. "It's a mystic riddle."

"Oh," said Johnny, "is the answer 'time'?"

"The answer is not 'time'!" I growled.

"'Man,' then—the answer's 'man,'" Johnny said.

"It's not that kind of riddle!"

"Oh."

I checked on Joey to see if he was still with me. It seemed that he was, but it was hard to tell with these two.

"It's like a mystery that will help you on your quest," I said.

"We're on a quest?" both boys asked.

"Life is a quest," I said. I gritted my teeth. "Just remember the riddle."

"Yes, sir!"

"Good," I said. "If ever we meet again I want to lay out some parameters. One: it will be an official consultation and will follow official wiseman rules, none of this bumping-into-each-other-on-the-astral-plane stuff."

Joey and Johnny agreed.

"Two: you will not beat me up."

"Yes, sir. Sorry, sir," they said.

"Seriously, I think you guys chipped a tooth. How do you chip an astral tooth? Oh, and before I forget. Boys?"

"Yes, sir."

"Don't eat the shrimp."

NINJA DON'T
HAVE SIDEKICKS

In which a young knight
embarks on a great journey,
again and again and again. . . .

The morning came, and everything was changed. Red Moon Clan—including Larry and Rufus, Rufus's weird metal boots, even the Stunion darts that had been stuck in Joey's and Johnny's skin—were gone. The broken windows had been fixed and the whole station had a just-tidied-up feel about it. Even the burning billboard had been replaced by a brand-new one. Flippy now told passersby, "Wanna be a NINJA? It's EASY!"

Joey was the first to stir. Stretching, he was surprised at how relatively well rested he felt. Johnny was slumped against Joey's shoulder, drooling.

The soft sound of metal hitting stone caught Joey's ear. At his feet was a moderate pile of change. A quarter spun, wobbled, and then joined the rest.

"It's a shame when ninjas can't find work," said a woman walking past. "You boys keep your chins up."

Joey felt as if his thoughts were glued to the inside of his skull. He shook his head, hoping it might jar a few of them loose. With luck they would fall into a pattern he could make sense of. He stood up and then immediately regretted it. Not only did it make the world spin, but he'd been the only thing keeping Johnny's head from hitting the pavement. So Johnny's head went down with a wince-inducing thunk.

"Johnny. *Johnny!* Wake up!"

"Monkeyshines!" Johnny said. He flipped to his feet and then fell right back down on his face, sending much of their money pile chiming away. Having gotten a larger dose of the octo-toxin, he had yet to fully recover.

"My arms!" Johnny said. "I've got no arms." His words were muffled because he was talking through a mouthful of change.

"You've got arms," Joey said, grabbing them and waving them about like pool noodles. "They're just not working right now."

Joey helped Johnny back up and massaged sensation into his limbs. Morning commuters, mostly made up of rangers, geologists, and resort attendants, continued to slide past the bedraggled ninjas.

"They think we're homeless," Joey said.

"Well, no wonder," Johnny said, finishing up his count of the change pile. "There's only twelve dollars and seventy-four cents here—where are we going to bed down for that?"

"You boys ninjas?"

The voice belonged to a gondola conductor. His cap was tipped back as he scratched his forehead. He didn't wait for them to answer.

"Is this your handiwork?" he said, jerking a thumb toward the back of his gondola. "He said something about ninjas."

"He who?" Joey asked.

"Ask him yourself, I've got a gondola to conduct." He turned back to his station, paused, and then looked over his shoulder. "Are you two some kinda hobo-ninjas?"

"We're the regular kind of ninja," Johnny said.

"Whatever. Look, deal with the mess in there. I'm not giving him another free trip."

Joey and Johnny boarded the gondola car and made their way past the rows of seats to the back. On the floor with the garbage and gum wrappers, and a year's accumulation of spilled mocha double lattes, was a body.

The figure was a little on the small side and dressed in an outfit that was one part medieval knight, one part sci-fi jumpsuit—a bizarre mixture of chain mail and spandex. He even wore a helmet complete with vented visor, at the top of which was a plume that looked like red smoke.

He wasn't dead, or sleeping. He had not risen because he had been bound with rope, a rough coil that wound around his body from shoulder to waist. It looked a little frayed, as if he had been working at it. Joey and Johnny guessed that it would've taken them less than five minutes to break free, but this boy had obviously been on the floor for quite some time.

Joey cleared his throat to get the trapped boy's attention. This came naturally to Joey because, as a ninja, he was quite used to people not noticing his approach. The boy looked up and greeted the two ninjas with a wide grin.

"Golly, are you here to rescue me?" When that got no immediate response he added, "I'm Knight-Lite, your new exchange student."

"Are you a spy?" Johnny asked. "Because if you are, we have to watch you go to the bathroom."

"Gosh, no," Knight-Lite said. "I'm a superhero!"

"You're a *superhero*?" Joey asked, with undisguised disgust.

"Well, more of a sidekick . . . ," Knight-Lite corrected.

"Even better."

". . . in training," Knight-Lite added.

Ninjas and superheroes do not get along. Superheroes consider ninjas to be, at best, one step above minions. That they are merely henchmen for supervillains and easily defeated even when fought in waves. SteamShovel Steve once defeated 275 ninjas with his shovel at only half-steam, leaving them all covered in a loose layer of topsoil. Ninjas, *real* ninjas, would point out that those other ninjas weren't really ninjas. Just thugs in black pajamas.

WISEMAN NOTE: SteamShovel Steve, the hero with the steam-powered shovel, should not be confused with the Anthropomorphic SteamShovel, a sentient man-shaped piece of heavy excavation equipment. The contest to determine which of them is the diggiest man alive still has no clear winner.

Ninjas don't like superheroes because in the world of ninjas, every ability is sought after and trained for. Ninjas go on quests for mystic knowledge, and they have their bodies pushed beyond the extreme to be able to do what they do. It takes years. Superheroes simply come from another dimension where everyone has laser eyes, or their uncle wills them a rocket-launching, talking car, or they get slapped in the face with a radioactive fish. They've done nothing to earn their power. Shortcuts are for losers. (Also maybe, just maybe, there's a touch of jealousy.)

Knight-Lite was untied and led outside. Pointing first to Knight-Lite and then to the gondola station's uncomfortable bench, Joey said, "Wait here. Private ninja meeting."

Joey quickly hoofed it over to the Red Moon sign and stood behind it, just out of view. Johnny waited next to their new sidekick until Joey gestured vigorously for him to follow.

"Johnny, this guy's definitely a—" Joey halted midsentence. "Hey!" he called over to Knight-Lite. "Do you have sound powers, echolocation, or have you ever been bitten by a mutant bat or something?"

"What?" Knight-Lite said. "Sometimes my helmet makes it hard to hear stuff."

"DO. YOU. HAVE. SUPER HEARING?" Joey yelled.

"Golly," Knight-Lite said, "I don't have *any* superpowers."

Joey spun back to Johnny. "This guy is soooooo a spy."

Johnny looked at Knight-Lite and then gave Joey a dubious look. "He doesn't look like a spy to me," said Johnny. "Anyway, he already told us he wasn't, which is good because I do not want bathroom duty."

"That's *exactly* what a spy would tell you," Joey said. "And you know what FangSwan always says."

Johnny did an eerily accurate impersonation: "'If any of you ever interrupt me I will grind your bones to powder, bake you into croutons, and sprinkle you on my salad. Which I will scrape into the garbage at the end of my meal, because I *hate* salad.'"

Joey shook off the image of becoming a discarded healthy alternative. "No," he said. "The other thing: 'Never trust a hero.' That's got to go double for superheroes."

Johnny disagreed. "Zato said we're ambassadors. Let's ambassadate."

Joey peeked around the corner to where Knight-Lite was still sitting, staring at the slowly descending gondola.

"You'd listen to Zato over the headmaster?"

Actually it was a silly question. Everyone would *rather* listen to Zato: he was more balanced and reasonable, and far less likely to kill you and then forget to even mention it in his journal. The question was, were you brave enough to listen to Zato?

"Come on," Johnny said. "Give the little guy a chance."

"Fine," Joey said. He stomped out from behind the sign and stood uncomfortably close to Knight-Lite. A chill morning breeze made the red plume of the sidekick's helmet drift into Joey's face. He brushed it away with disdain.

"Greetings, I am Joey. This is Johnny—"

"Hello." Johnny waved with both hand and dooley-bopper.

"It is an 'honor' to be your 'escorts' and 'aides' during your time at our school," Joey said in a tone that suggested the opposite. "Let us begin our journey. Don't try any funny stuff."

"Don't worry. I won't," Knight-Lite said. "I haven't taken my quip classes yet. Is that the kind of thing I can learn at ninja school?"

Joey stared up at the heavens and wondered which of the old ninja masters were shaking their heads in disgust. It's not my fault, he thought, but he was certain the clouds were looking down in disapproval.

It was going to be a long walk.

A TEA PARTY
IN THE WOODS

In which Johnny learns about
the inner workings of squirrels and
Joey does battle with a pastry.

The climb back up the mountain was a particular hardship for Knight-Lite. His work with his mentor, Night-Knight, mostly included tinkering with or repairing the knight's various bits of techno-weaponry. He also occasionally got kidnapped by various members of Night-Knight's rogues' gallery. So far there hadn't been much call for running up and down a mountain; you didn't get a lot of exercise being tied to a chair. But that didn't stop him from trying to have a chat with his new best buddies.

"So . . . *gasp* . . . what . . . *choke* . . . do you fellas do for fun . . . around here . . . ?"

"Apparently we drag deadweight around the forest while listening to monkey chatter," said Joey, not bothering to look back.

"Oh, golly!" said Knight-Lite in between breaths. "I once put together a device that lets you understand monkeys! It was okay for a while." A stray branch slapped him in the visor, making him flail. "Monkeys spend an awful lot of time talking about poop."

Johnny lent Knight-Lite a hand with some geraniums that were trying to tangle about his legs. Even flowers wanted to tie him up. "I like smashing stuff with my hammer," said Johnny. "I also like naming my hammer. He's Timothy Poundwell today!"

"Why Timothy Poundwell?" asked Knight-Lite.

Johnny pondered the question very seriously. "Well, it sounds British, and the last time I smashed something with it, the *smoosh* sound came out with an English accent."

Knight-Lite nodded in complete understanding. "Oh, Night-Knight lets me name all his new gizmos! There's the Freezy Flash Poppers, the Electro-Spang-Tangler, the Gyro-Laser-Lasso, and Mean Joe!"

"Oh! What does Mean Joe do?"

"It makes you think you're being stalked by an angry badger. It's tough to commit a crime when you're expecting a badger to jump you."

Joey could stand it no longer. "What happens when you don't have your gizmos to save you? What do you do when your Electro-Dingle-Doodle-Hopper fizzles out?"

"*Hmmm*," considered Knight-Lite. "In my case, I get tied to a chair and keep the villain busy with conversation."

The reply made Joey angrier. It was hard to insult a guy who kept insulting himself. "Well, FangSwan isn't going to let you have any doohickeys here. The closest thing we have to a high-tech weapon is a pair of nunchucks! Good luck not knocking yourself out!"

"Oh, I've used those! I invented a pair of electrochucks."

"Does *everything* you use have to have the word 'electro' in it?" Joey spat.

"No," said Knight-Lite, "we also use words like 'plasmo,' 'incendiary,' 'sonic,' and—" He stopped midsentence as a fern tried to tie him to a tree.

Joey sliced him free with a lazy flick of his katana. "You're not even going to survive lunch."

"Yeah," said Knight-Lite

cheerily, "particularly if there's dairy. I'm completely intolerant."

"I'm intolerant of pirates, horses, and February," said Johnny.

"Why horses?" asked Knight-Lite.

"It's their nostrils—they steam! What's going on inside those things?" said Johnny.

Joey was beginning to feel as if he'd wandered into the wrong story. He was supposed to be the hero in a *ninja* tale with some fighting and sharp dangerous things flying at his head. Now he was having a chat in the woods and birds were trying to perch on his shoulder. All he needed was a talking squirrel in a hat and Joey would be in a fairy tale.

At that moment a bear lumbered out of the woods onto the trail in front of them.

"Oh, a bear!" he said, perking up. "Those are dangerous!"

The bear was wearing a waistcoat, and he looked embarrassed about it.

"Oh, come *on*. I can't fight that!" There were more animals wandering out of the woods wearing various bits of clothing. Three bunnies wearing little top hats wiggled their noses in Joey's direction. They were an insult to everything ninja.

"Johnny, are you seeing this too, or did I just get knocked out again?" asked Joey.

"What?" said Johnny. "They're just some animals in the woods, that's where animals come from."

"Johnny! Look at what they're wearing!"

"Well, yeah, they're a little overdressed for the occasion, but I don't see . . ."

"They're *animals*! Any dressed is overdressed for them."

Joey headed into the trees, following the line of confused woodland creatures. Johnny and Knight-Lite trailed along. This wasn't adventure, but at least it counted as a mystery. Maybe this was the work of some sort of forest demon. Demons put up a decent fight. As they headed deeper into the woods, Joey could just make out a voice coming through a clearing ahead. It sounded . . . it sounded like someone trying to sound elegant. "Oh, theeere you are, Mrs. Darbyshire! Let me pour you a cup of tea. *Dooo* take care to wipe your feet on the rug."

Joey knew that sound. It was the sound of a tea party! Joey's heart quickened. It seemed his wish for

99

danger had been answered.

Oh yes, *danger!* There are few things so horrifying as an invite to a ninja tea party. In many ways they look just like the sort of tea party you might be picturing: spoons making tinkly sounds on china cups, tiny little sandwiches, adorable muffins, and ridiculous hats. But it's the rules that can reduce a proud warrior to a quivering mess. At last count there are 147,583 specific rules of conduct at a proper ninja tea party. Everything from the angle of your wrist during pouring, the height of your elbow while drinking, how you unfold your napkin, and how many times you tinkle your spoon against the cup. Now, breaking a rule at a standard tea party can be embarrassing, but it's very rarely fatal. At a ninja tea party the host is obligated to add an element of danger for every rule you break. Grip your teacup wrong and maybe you'll be slipped the poisoned sandwich. Left elbow not facing the setting sun? You get the spring-loaded dart in your muffin. And throughout this dance with death you are expected to be agonizingly polite at all times. Even while checking your sandwich for bombs.

Ninja tea parties are to be avoided, and if they can't be, they are to be survived.

Joey pulled Johnny and Knight-Lite into a huddle. "It's a tea party, guys!" Johnny drew a deep intake of breath. Knight-Lite beamed in delight. "Stop beaming in delight, Knight-Lite—it's not what you think. Here's how we're going to survive this; left elbow facing the setting sun, wrist cocked at thirty degrees while drinking but forty degrees while pouring, say 'please' and 'thank you' after everything the host says, no more than twelve tinkles of the teaspoon . . ." Joey went on for fifteen minutes. "Okay!" he said when he finished the list. "Everybody got that?"

"Got it!" said Johnny.

"Sure thing," said Knight-Lite.

Joey got as close as he could to the owner of the voice they had heard. He could see a large, imposing figure seated on a tree stump. Surrounding the figure were a host of cakes and little sandwiches. Obviously each and every one held a deadly secret. At the figure's feet was a loose circle of dressed-up animals gazing with interest at a delicious-looking cake the figure was holding. What kind of a madman was this?

"I *dooooo* hope you shall try the apple crumb tart, Mr. Dribblesbottom," said the figure with its false poshness. Mr. Dribblesbottom was apparently a squirrel in a crude tie. He clearly didn't know what he was doing, because he accepted the cake with two paws *and* his tail was at the wrong angle. Plus, he didn't check the cake for darts before shoving it into his mouth.

"Mr. Dribblesbottom, *nooooo!*" cried Johnny,

leaping out from behind Joey with his hammer in midswing. Knight-Lite leapt into the fray as well, just

as Johnny's hammer buried itself in the sandwich table. Cucumber sandwiches exploded in every direction.

"Watch the finger sandwiches!" cried Joey, unsheathing his sword and disarming the teapot with one stroke.

Knight-Lite caught a sandwich in the face. "Aaaagh, there's cucumber in my eeeeyyyee!"

"Johnny, save Knight-Lite!"

"I can't, Joey, I'm saving the squirrel!" Johnny had Mr. Dribblesbottom by the tail and was trying to stick a finger down his throat.

"Don't worry about me!" squealed Knight-Lite, clutching his cucumber-smeared eye and pounding off into the forest. "One of the top-hat bunnies snagged a muffin and I'm going to save it! YAAAAAAAAaaaaaaaaaaa . . . !"

Joey got to work disarming the remaining desserts, his sword flashing as he pulverized an army of pastries. . . .

"What are you three doing?" yelped a voice that had lost all trace of its fake elegance.

Joey stopped, a mangled crumpet hanging from the tip of his sword.

Johnny stopped, his finger up to the third knuckle in Mr. Dribblesbottom's mouth.

Knight-Lite stopped yelling "yaaaaa." It wasn't because of the voice—he'd just accidentally gagged and bound himself to a tree.

Peoni stood looking stricken amid the wreckage of her tea party.

"Wah . . . Peoni?" said Joey.

"Ten thousand curses! I almost did it perfectly! Why did you attack my sandwiches?" she shouted, kicking the ruined remains of the cake at her feet.

"Um," began Joey, "because we wanted to *live*?"

"It's not a real tea party!" Peoni sputtered, kneading her forehead with the tips of her fingers. Looking up at Johnny, she said, "Johnny, could you please get your finger out of that squirrel? The cake wasn't poisoned."

Johnny put the squirrel down. "Sorry, Mr. Dribblesbottom, I meant well." The squirrel yacked on Johnny and ran off.

Joey said, "What is going on here? Why are you having"—he choked the words out—"a tea party?"

Peoni sighed and stepped out of her bulky tea armor. Joey was glad to see that she was dressed like a proper ninja underneath. "Guys, if I tell you what I'm doing, you're going to join in and turn it into one of your wacky, zany adventures! It'll be called *Joey and Johnny the Ninjas and the Blah Blah Tea Party Blah Blah!*"

"Well, we're not going to sell it with *that* title!" said Johnny.

"That. Doesn't. Matter," Peoni said, punctuating each word with a finger poke to Johnny's chest, "because this time it's going to be called *Peoni the Ninja and the Mysterious Thing She Can't Tell You About 'Cause It's a Super-Dangerous Secret and You Guys Might Mess It Up!*"

"That's a bit wordy for a title," said Johnny, "but I still kinda want to read it."

"Yeah, me too," added Joey. "Let's skip to the last page, where Peoni tells her pals the big secret!"

"Is that your exchange student?" she asked, clearly ready to change the subject.

Joey looked embarrassed. "Uh, yeah . . . I kinda thought it was going to be a ninja."

"Well, I bet FangSwan kinda thought that too . . . and you DO know he organized a welcoming party for *two nights ago?*"

"What?!" said Joey, turning pale. "When has Fang-Swan ever welcomed ANYTHING?"

"Two nights ago, apparently, but you guys weren't there...."

Johnny asked, "Peoni, why do you keep saying 'two nights ago'?"

"Because you've been gone for two days."

Time flies when you're chemically sedated. Funny how when you wake up in the morning you automatically assume that *only* one day has passed. Strangely, Joey didn't feel like laughing.

"Johnny! Get Knight-Lite untied! We have to go *now!*"

They made their way through the darkening forest at a dead run. Joey and Johnny each had one of Knight-Lite's elbows so they could just drag him through the vines and prickly bushes that wanted him. A few forest beasts tried to do battle with them, but there was no time for fun. They barreled through these dangers with a few quick thumps of Johnny's hammer.

"Sorry," said Johnny over his shoulder at a deeply offended troll. "Maybe later!"

They careened up the stairs to the school's entrance and burst into the receiving corridor.

Everyone was there. *Everyone!*

Knight-Lite sank to his knees, holding his sides. Joey and Johnny gasped for breath, taking in the scene in front of them. Every KFA student stood in a massive circle surrounding them, staring at Joey and

Johnny through bloodshot eyes. A few were still clinging to banners that said "Welcome, new student, we are
watching you" and "Don't try anything stupid." The
floor was littered with deflated balloons.

"Oh, hello!" said a bright, cheerful voice. "Look,
students! Flumpy and Dodo made it to our party!
Would you like some shrimp, Flumpy and Dodo?
There's shrimp!" FangSwan gestured to a table that was
emitting a powerful aroma of the sea. The shrimp was
covered in flies and the crab legs didn't look any better.

THE WISDOM
OF FANGSWAN

In which FangSwan does something scary
in a cruel and heartless manner.

"I . . . I . . . ," struggled Joey through heaving breaths. "I can explain, Headmaster Fa—"

Vice Principal Zato gave a quick wave and a shake of his head. FangSwan had been waiting two days to deliver his welcoming speech. The longer he waited, the more the speech ripened in FangSwan's twisted brain. Now it would burst forth and all anyone could do was hunker down and bear it.

"Students," began FangSwan brightly, "I don't like any of you. If one day I am reading the newspaper and there is an article about one of you having been eaten by a large, terrible thing, I will switch to the sports page and read about which football group made the most basket scores. Each one of you is as unimportant to me as a decorative button cover. Why would you want to cover your buttons? Why didn't you just buy a shirt with buttons you like? *Are you a fool?*"

He paused so his students could digest this.

"What is important to me is the name of ninja. It should inspire fear! It should inspire awe! It should be a name so powerful you cannot write it without your piece of paper burning, or say it without your tongue leaping from your mouth and running away! Ninjas are not action figures, they do not decorate your lunch boxes, they are not pretty colors for your *cartoon television sets*!"

This last bit was said with such venom that every fly on the banquet table died in unison. Their bodies hitting the floor sounded like a brief gentle rain. Fang-Swan inhaled for the last part.

"I care that when each of you leaves this school you will either leave in utter disgrace *or you will leave as a ninja!*" The word "ninja" reverberated down the hallway and out across the mountaintop, making trees sway.

"Now," he said, fixing his gaze on the three boys huddled at his feet, "does anyone have anything to add?"

Knight-Lite stood up and unfolded a sheet of paper. FangSwan stood with his hands upraised, the fingers spread like claws. Only his eyeballs moved to follow the paper the tiny sidekick held out to him.

It was a fairly decent drawing of Flippy the Ninja.

He snatched the drawing from Knight-Lite's hand and quickly passed it to his blind vice principal. "What *is* this?" he said.

Zato touched the drawing. "I believe it's a drawing of Flippy the Ninja."

"What is a 'Flippy the Ninja'?" asked FangSwan.

"I just wanted to prove that I can belong at your school, Mr. FangSwan, sir," bubbled Knight-Lite. "Now, how many weeks exactly will it take for me to become a ninja?"

"*Weeeeeeeks?!*" said FangSwan. "It takes a lifetime to

become a ninja, but *good news*. In your case, that could be measured in minutes."

Joey stepped forward and yanked Knight-Lite behind him. "We can explain, Headmaster FangSwan."

All of FangSwan's considerable malevolence shifted to Joey. "Students, we are all being treated to the Flumpy and Dodo story hour. Let us listen as if their lives depend on it."

THE FLUMPY AND DODO STORY HOUR

In which we learn about how enormously
important storytellers are and how
they should be treated with great
respect and expensive presents.

FangSwan had kept the entire school waiting in the receiving corridor for two days and two nights. The first night wasn't so bad, and they had the smell of delicious seafood to comfort them. But as the night wore on and then the day and then the night again, the students of KFA began to lose their minds. It didn't help that FangSwan stood without moving, arms folded comfortably on his chest and a grand welcoming smile on his face that didn't flicker once. No matter how tired they got, there was no possible way to sleep with FangSwan's grinning face staring at them. And if they *did* nod off, FangSwan made it clear he had a handsome wooden box filled to the brim with snuggly scorpions that he would share with them. The only two seemingly unaffected by the ordeal were Vice Principal Zato, who snoozed silently behind his dark glasses, and Brad, who smiled warmly and didn't move a muscle. The rest stood and turned ever-darker thoughts toward Joey and Johnny.

This was Joey and Johnny's audience.

"Um . . . ," began Joey. Good start. Hundreds of bleary, red eyes turned toward him.

Johnny nudged him in the ribs. "Open with a joke!"

"Red Moon . . . ," began Joey.

"Ha! Good one!" said Johnny.

FangSwan stalked toward them both. He got so close his eyebrows poked Joey in the eyeball. "What did you say?"

How a hush managed to fall over an already silent room is beyond me, but it happened.

"Uh . . . Red Moon," Joey said again, his voice muffled by FangSwan's beard.

"Could an ant block your path?" asked FangSwan.

"How big is the ant?" asked Johnny.

"A normal-size ant!" hissed FangSwan.

"No, sir. . . . An ant couldn't block my path," said Joey.

"How about a noodle? Could a noodle give you a

wedgie?" continued FangSwan.

"How big is the . . ."

"SHUT UP, FLUMPY!"

"I thought *he* was Flumpy . . . ," muttered Johnny.

"Sir, a noodle couldn't stop me, and neither could a Moony," said Joey. "But . . . they had things we haven't seen before and they were up to something strange in the forest!"

It was no secret that FangSwan considered all the forested areas surrounding his school to belong solely to him. A squirrel couldn't bury a nut without Fang-Swan knowing its exact location. Sometimes he'd take it and rebury it for fun.

FangSwan took great pride in never being caught unawares. Joey desperately wanted the Red Moon incident to remain a secret, but right now only a greater outrage could deflect the headmaster's unwanted attention.

Joey watched the gears turn in FangSwan's mind. They made a sound like cogs in some medieval torture device. With a metallic click a decision was reached. "Zato, did you know of this?"

"I have been looking into the matter," answered Zato calmly.

"Come with me," said FangSwan. As the two left he spoke to the room. "Students, enjoy the party. Eat some shrimp."

The dazed students sagged and turned to gaze at the table of rotting seafood. As a unit they turned back to stare at Joey and Johnny, who looked relieved and well rested.

"We sure dodged a nunchuck that time, didn't we, Joey!" said Johnny, oblivious to the rotting shrimp and angry eyes.

Joey understood what was going to happen next, but by then it was too late.

Sleeping isn't a big part of life at KFA, but even ninjas have to do it on occasion. For that purpose the students had little wooden huts anchored to the side of the mountain. Each hut held two students and could be entered by a square hole cut in the floor. There were no ropes or ladders, so sleep was a reward that had to be earned by an arduous climb up the sheer rock wall. Ting had never even seen the inside of his sleeping hut. If you wanted to invite him to breakfast, you needed to shake the mulberry bush he huddled in.

Johnny pointed it out to Knight-Lite as they headed for bed. Anything to distract them from the horrific stench that surrounded the three boys like a green putrescent cloud. They had managed to dodge the first two waves of the seafood storm, but the third, fourth, and fifth courses got past their defenses. The boys had actual visible cartoon stink lines coming off them. To Joey's eternal shame, it was Brad who put a stop to the attack.

"Sorry I couldn't save you fellas sooner," he had said. "I was on the astral plane helping an Indian princess find her missing body!"

Brad had had an adventure while standing in the wrathful gaze of their headmaster. Why didn't *he* smell like the underside of a fisherman's boat? Also, Brad apparently knew all about the astral plane.

They reached the base of the cliff where their sleeping hut jutted out from the rock far above them. Joey and Johnny smoothly raced up the wall, bouncing from handhold to toehold. Knight-Lite stood at the bottom looking up at them. Knights are not designed for climbing—it's one of the reasons you don't have to worry about one leaping out of a tree at you. Joey would have been content to let Knight-Lite find a mulberry bush next to Ting's, but Johnny was having none of that. They snagged some sheets from their room and strung a few together to make some rope.

"That's a decent bit of rope you made. It would have kept me in a chair for a few days!" said Knight-Lite approvingly when he hauled himself the rest of the way into the hut. It had little in the way of furnishings, just a couple of woven mats to sack out on and a few posters on Johnny's side.

Knight-Lite looked with interest at Johnny's posters. "You watch *Diddums the Talking Teacup and His Army of Battle Cutlery?*"

"I did when I lived on the island!" said Johnny. "Though I stopped watching when Diddums got too gritty and realistic."

"You lived on an island?"

It wouldn't have occurred to Johnny to mention this as a point of interest, but Johnny didn't just live on an island—he was the prince of one. Badoni Dony was a tiny volcanic island lost deep in the Pacific Ocean. In the native language its name meant: "It's just a name, it doesn't mean anything." Johnny's great-great-times-ten-grandfather founded the island back when people were beginning to realize that this "writing" thing was more than a passing fad. He became obsessed with the island's population of strange cave squids and soon discovered that their ink had properties far beyond just writing and drawing. Since then Johnny's family had guarded the secrets of the squid and were hailed as monarchs by the island's native inhabitants.

As far as monarchs went they weren't terrible. They instituted the three-day workweek and had a biweekly festival honoring whatever they'd been thinking of while crafting the calendar. This explains the festival of little boxes and the festival of "I screwed this page up and now I have to start all over."

Johnny told Knight-Lite about meeting the island's famous children's book author, Arugalla Picklebee. She was renowned for books such as *The Stump Full of Sporks That Know My Name* and *Wiggeldy-Spiggeldy Spiders Are Borrowing My Teeth*. Critics the world over thought that her imagination was second to none. The truth was, she lived too close to the island's volcanic vents and had gone completely mad. She was confused as to why publishers kept sending her money for pages from her daily journal.

"Arugalla Picklebee?" said Knight-Lite. "Is she the same woman who wrote that song 'Chimney Pup'—"

"GAH!" interrupted Joey. Johnny looked stricken. "Don't mention that . . . please."

Knight-Lite, confused, cast a wary eye at Johnny and changed the subject. "How about you, Joey? Where are you from?"

Joey would have preferred to sleep, but Johnny needed to be pulled off his current thought-path. "My dad is a coal miner," explained Joey. "He . . . uh . . . didn't really love that I wanted to be a ninja. But my grandfather was a ninja and he didn't really love that my dad wanted to be a coal miner." He knitted his brow for a moment, thinking. "And I think *his* father was a coal miner. . . ."

Joey's father had done his best to see his son in a nice, normal job. He'd taken little Joey along with him to work, given him a tiny pickax and a helmet with a light. Johnny's parents had tried much the same thing. They sent him along with the squid wranglers and gave him his own net and squid-milking kit. But both boys had had the same experience: they'd wiped their eyes clean after a hard day's mining or milking, and discovered their very first ninja masks: Joey's was made of coal dust and Johnny's of squid ink.

Johnny wanted to talk TV again and Knight-Lite was ready to match him show for show.

"*The Twinkle-Pants Raccoons?*"

"Oh, man! That show was the worst! What about *My Talking Horse Who Turned into a Hydrofoil?*"

"How did that show go for three seasons? But I *lived* for *Farmer MacGregor's Battle 'Copter!*"

"I know they were different species, but I really thought he was gonna get together with his cow. I kinda wanted it to happen."

"I'm with you on that, pal; Bessie was a sweet girl. But his own chickens were the bad guys all along?"

"*The Justice Swim Team?*"

"Yuck! *The Pie and Ape Mystery Hour?*"

"Ha!"

"What about *Practical Advice Guy?*"

Johnny and Knight-Lite had forgotten Joey was in the room, so it was a bit of a shock to hear him speak.

"Who?" said Johnny and Knight-Lite.

"My dad told me stories about Practical Advice Guy. He had that catchphrase"—Joey cleared his voice—"*Always make sure to have the . . .* right tool for the job . . ." Joey trailed off as he noticed that Johnny and Knight-Lite weren't saying it along with him. "I thought everybody knew about Practical Advice Guy and his *tool belt full of well-maintained tools!* My dad said he was more popular than Mickey Mouse!"

"Uh," said Johnny, "I think maybe your dad made that up, Joey."

"What? No! My dad didn't know how to make stuff up!"

"Clearly," said Johnny.

Knight-Lite noticed that Joey looked upset. "Well . . . can you tell us one of his adventures?"

"Sure!" said Joey, cheering up for the first time all day. "I'll tell you my favorite one! This is the one where Practical Advice Guy goes to assemble some two-by-fours into a rectangular frame, but he doesn't have the proper miter guide for his table saw and he *knew* he was never gonna get a proper forty-five-degree angle on . . ."

Johnny and Knight-Lite fell asleep immediately, but somewhere in the depths of their dreams they felt that they should oil their guide bearings and clear their dust extractors.

11

BATTLE CRYING

In which the boys watch the death of theater.

The warrior leapt up, his wooden mask glowering down with a terrifying grimace. He held a kusari-gama in his black-gloved hands. Each end of the weapon whispered a different terrible promise to its victim: a viciously sharp sickle on one side and a black spinning chain on the other. The spinning blur seemed to sing their laments as it grew closer and closer.

"The night shall drink your *terror!*" the figure shouted from atop his desk.

"He's going to kill us!" Knight-Lite shouted. His voice was followed by the clackety whirl of his wrist shield deploying.

"Nice to know I've still got the goods," Sensei Ren-bow said, laughing his little laugh. He returned the

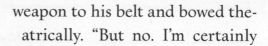

weapon to his belt and bowed the-atrically. "But no. I'm certainly not going to murder any-one, except"—he paused for effect—"perhaps"—another pause—"with my critique of your battle cries."

He hung the Noh demon mask on the wall next to the others with a supreme sense of self-satisfaction. Other than Knight-Lite, who applauded, the class was not impressed. They'd seen it before.

Sensei Renbow taught Theatrical Arts and Philosophy, and he often made a point of turning one into the other. Students were routinely dragged up to the small stage in the front of the class, given a costume, mask, and script, and suddenly made to be part of the day's lesson.

Often the performances descended into simple morality plays whose central goal was to reinforce one of Renbow's many Confucius-like clichés. The plays also managed to feature Renbow himself as either the lead hero or villain, occasionally performing both roles complete with costume changes. The students played the leftover roles and bit parts.

The end of the year always culminated in a full production in which every student had a part to play. Last year's was a three-hour piece titled *Silence, I Name Thee Friend*, during which the only two words spoken (both by Sensei Renbow) were "Begin" and "Finis."

"The battle cry I recited for you at the beginning of class was a favorite of Master Kain Grimstroke the Unwashed. Terrifying? Yes. But also flawed. Can anyone tell me what was wrong with that battle cry?" Renbow put a hand to his ear and awaited answers.

"Terror isn't a liquid?"

"The night might not be thirsty?"

Sensei Renbow shook his head. "No, no. Anyone? Well, the answer is in the word 'night.' It wasn't a very versatile cry. What would happen if you had to fight someone during the daytime?"

Renbow scanned his students' faces and said, "Where's Ting? Normally he's quite good at this." It was true. Theatrical Arts was Ting's favorite. It was the one class that didn't put him in the hospital.

Johnny muttered, "Ting would've pointed out that sometimes terror *can* be a liquid."

"Ting won't be joining us, Master Renbow," Peoni said glumly.

Joey had discovered the news that morning on the

way to breakfast. He had poked his head under Ting's mulberry bush and found everything gone except for a note. All it said was "Sorry, guys," with a drawing of Flippy the Ninja. It was his best so far, but it still wasn't great.

Breakfast was a sullen affair in which Peoni took an uncustomary three waffles to the face. As if sensing weakness, the lunch ladies seemed to focus more food in their direction than usual. By the time the meal was over, Johnny had enough pats of butter on him that he looked as if he was wearing a giraffe costume. Joey managed to dodge everything except one full trough of piping-hot maple syrup. Afterward he just sat, stuck to his chair. He smelled delicious for the rest of the day. Knight-Lite, new to the cafeteria, spent the entire time bouncing food off his wrist shield and screaming, "Why do those horrible women want to kill us with food?"

Joey and Johnny's spirits lifted a little during fight class, until a particularly well-spun nunchuck connected with Knight-Lite's helmet, creating a perfect *ting* that rang through the classroom. A moment of silence followed, and they remembered what they had lost.

"It's not like he's dead," Peoni said. In some ways it

was worse. He had joined Red Moon Clan. Ting had *decided* to become a Moony. How do you process that? They had always taken great pleasure in mocking the Moonies, but now that their friend was one of them it was no longer as funny.

Their glum mood continued as they shuffled along the school's hallways for their second session with Sensei Renbow. They'd all spent a late night writing battle cries and were mumbling the words to themselves as they walked. Their teacher had promised them a special surprise, and that was made apparent when they walked into the classroom. The lights in the room were extinguished and the curtains were drawn. Paper sky lanterns powered by little candles bobbed and floated about, casting a shifting light on the walls and ceiling.

"Yesterday, class, we discussed words. Today we discuss feelings, which are so much more important," Renbow said from a shadowy corner of the room. "Pick your target and dispatch it with the raw emotional power of your battle cry."

Joey didn't need further invitation. He drew his sword in a smooth motion, shouting *"Run! Run! I will dine on your entrails!"* and sliced one of the paper targets in half.

Joey was celebrating with an exuberant "Yesss!" when his teacher interrupted with a clap. "Yes, congratulations, Joey. You bravely cut some paper with a sword. Perhaps you are too advanced for this class!"

There was enough sarcasm in Renbow's tone to bend cutlery. Joey did not miss it and hushed up immediately, ignoring Johnny's attempt to high-five him. Renbow continued with a lighter tone. "Your foe is not rattled by the words of your battle cry, but rather by the emotion behind it. Focus your passion. I want you to use the steel in your voice to cut down the target, not the steel in your weapon." He adjusted his long, flowing sleeves and fixed his gaze on one of the bobbing lanterns.

"I dispatch thee with my *feelings*!" he spat in a voice that crackled through the room and set everyone's arm hairs on alert.

The lantern's candle flickered and went out, dropping the paper balloon dead to the floor. The class wasn't used to being impressed by their drama teacher, and they let out a soft "whoa."

Joey took another try, this time extending the *s* in "entrailsssss" for as long as his puffed-out cheeks could manage. The tiny blast of air that escaped his mask made the lantern spin prettily, but it did not put out the candle.

"That's air, Joey, not emotion," said Renbow.

The students around the room set themselves to putting out their targets. FuShoe made a near hit with her "I'll peel you like a grape!" The candle definitely flickered.

Peoni attempted to put out her lantern with a heartfelt "I miss Ting!" but it had no effect at all.

"You cannot dispatch an enemy with sadness, my dear girl," Renbow said, "no matter how deeply it's felt." He touched her shoulder gently. "You need to use your anger and passion for this exercise."

She tried again with "Ting's an idiot!" The candle flickered.

Two boys named Whistler and Spratt attempted to take on their lantern with a combined "Release the fury!" Their lantern went out, but only because they'd crashed into it.

A whip-thin boy named Trimil threw out, "I'm gonna stab you with my stabby-thing!" The candle ignored him.

Brad picked a lantern and the class instinctively stopped to watch. His first attempt—"Stop, villain!"— had no effect whatsoever. Joey was unable to suppress a smile, but with Brad's second attempt—"I said *stop!*"— both the candle and Joey's smile flickered out.

Joey smacked his fist and said, "Braaaad!" A lantern nearby crumpled to the ground but he didn't notice.

Knight-Lite tried "For king and country!!" It had no

effect on the lantern, but Renbow gave him an encouraging nod and said, "Very European!"

It was Johnny's turn. He stuck his chin out at the lantern he'd chosen and blew a puff of air at his dooley-bopper to get it out of his eyes. His empty hands flexed, itching for his hammer. He took a breath and shouted, "Ut OH, you poked the BUNNY!"

All the remaining lanterns puffed out and clattered to the ground.

"*What?*" said Sensei Renbow in a tone that required no acting embellishment. "*That* is the phrase you feel emotionally passionate about?!"

From the darkness the stunned students heard Johnny say, "Well, yeah, it's only the best catchphrase ever!"

"Johnny," came Renbow's reply, "that was . . . that was so very—you." They could hear him rubbing his brow. "Let's have some light!"

The window shades were opened and afternoon daylight returned to the room. Sensei Renbow placed himself center stage and gave his class a polite round of applause.

"I thank you all for your performances. I must now think upon them. I suggest you do the same."

With a flourish of his loose robes, the sensei took his notes and regally glided behind a small paper screen that he used for wardrobe changes and coffee breaks.

The students broke into a low chatter.

"Okay," said Joey, "what is up with poking the bunny? I've been hearing you yell that for a year now."

"Yeah," Peoni said. "I always thought I was hearing you wrong."

"It's only from the best show ever!" Johnny said. "Come on, you know . . ."

"No, we don't," Joey and Peoni said.

"I think I might have heard that one," Knight-Lite chimed in.

"*RabbitShark!*" Johnny said with awe and wonder. "Everybody's watching it."

WISEMAN NOTE: No. They weren't.

RabbitShark was a live-action television show that ran in the eighties. It featured an innocent little girl and the horrible abomination that she loved. The title character was, as his name implied, half rabbit and half shark. Together Emily and RabbitShark traveled the world and solved water-themed crimes. At the end of every episode some bad guy generally fell into water and got eaten while Emily cheered, "Ut OH! You poked the BUNNY!"

It opened with a Nielsen rating of 1.1 and went down from there. Eventually it became the show that the other networks would put their weakest shows against just to give them a boost. The plots were formulaic. The sets were poorly built. The acting was atrocious. The RabbitShark suit was routinely malfunctioning or obviously damaged from previous takes. It was unquestionably too violent for prime-time TV.

Johnny's island, Badoni Dony, had gotten cable only four years ago. The local cable company is very small and at first didn't have the cash to buy any of the more popular shows. It was limited to airing the most undesirable and therefore least expensive programming. At the top of that list was *RabbitShark*. For whatever reason, it was a hit and became the most-watched show in all of Badoni Dony.

Joey said, "Maybe you dreamed it. The line between imagination and reality has always been pretty thin for you, Johnny."

"Seriously," Johnny asked, "you've never heard of it?"

"This is one of those times when I worry about you, Johnny," Peoni said.

"It's a *real* show," Johnny insisted.

Both Joey and Peoni started to back away slowly, hands held up in a position of surrender.

"Feh! You don't know what you're missing."

Knight-Lite got an idea. "Maybe I can find it," he said.

"How?"

The sidekick proudly lifted his arm, showing off the high-tech metal bracer wrapped around it. It seemed to be made of hammered steel, similar to a knight's polished helmet. There was a series of nearly invisible buttons on its smooth surface.

They already knew it could unfold into a round shield in the blink of an eye, but when Knight-Lite ran his fingers across it, it started to glow.

"INPUT," it said in a pleasant but flat female voice. The ninjas gasped.

"*RabbitShark*," Knight-Lite said. "Television show."

"COMPUTING."

"You've got a magic voice," Johnny said.

"Gosh, no," Knight-Lite said. "This is my holographic computer. Night-Knight built it from scratch. Besides the shield, it can do tons of stuff. Internet browsing, video and audio communication, day planning, note-taking, and it can even glow at night because"—there was a pause where he tried to say nothing more, but honesty got the better of him—"sometimes I'm a little scared of the dark."

"Knight-Lite has a night light—go figure," Joey said.

Peoni elbowed Joey in the ribs. "I'm sure it's great," she said.

"COMPUTING," the computer said again.

"Who's the magic voice?" asked Johnny.

"Oh, that's MERLIN, short for Micro-Engineered

Robotic Luminescent Intelligent Nulti-tool."

"'Luminescent'?" said Joey.

"'Nulti-tool'?" asked Peoni.

Knight-Lite looked embarrassed. "Yeah. You see, it, uh—glows and uh—Night-Knight *really* wanted it to be called MERLIN. He has a whole medieval castle–theme thing going."

"Why not just call it 'Mobile Elite Reinforced Long-Range Intelligence Network'?"

Everyone stopped dead and looked at Johnny. Knight-Lite frantically scribbled it down.

"Nice one, Johnny. Did you pull that off the top of your head?" Joey asked.

"Sure, it's not hard," said Johnny. "How about 'Magically Enraged Rhinos Living in Nebraska,' or . . ."

Peoni jumped in. "Or 'Many Emotive Rebel Llamas Instantly Nude.'"

"Nice!" said Johnny. "What about 'Marmosets Eat R—"

Joey cut him off. "Okay, okay. Enough. We're impressed."

Peoni and Johnny put their heads together, continuing to whisper new ones, until MERLIN chirped, "THIRTY-SEVEN RESULTS FOUND."

"Show results," Knight-Lite said. Despite the clunky audio interface, the holographic display was amazing.

Thin lines glowed across the surface of the gauntlet in red, green, and blue. Projected lines of light met two inches above Knight-Lite's arm to form a translucent display. His finger pushed against the ghostly screen and scrolled effortlessly down the results page.

"Yep, I remember it now," Knight-Lite said. "There's even a clip from the pilot on TwitFace."

He pressed PLAY and a little icon of a TV began to fill with color.

Joey grimaced and said, "This is exactly the kind of stuff the Moonies were using. You heard FangSwan. I'm sure *superheroes* use this kind of stuff every day, but it goes against all things ninja. We should—"

"Shut up, it's starting!" Johnny cried.

137

138

"You watch the death of theater while in *my* class-room!" boomed Sensei Renbow in a scandalized vibrato. The four students looked up from Knight-Lite's screen in guilty surprise. Their teacher shook with rage; tears threatened the corners of his eyes. "Report to Vice Principal Zato's office at once. Tell him you skinned and ate the spirit of culture right in front of me!"

Joey cringed. No one liked to get in trouble at KFA. On the path to becoming a ninja, many of the lessons could be considered torturous. Punishments could be murder.

The three ninjas had experience with punish-ment and no wish to repeat it. Johnny once spent an entire afternoon as an archery target. Peoni and Joey were once penalized together for returning fire on the lunch ladies after one of them hit Ting with a still-flaming baked Alaska. Stripped of his ninja toe-boots, Joey had to run across a carpet made of living porcupines. Peoni had to wrangle those porcupines while wearing a blindfold, a job made significantly harder after Joey's second belly flop whipped them into a rage.

Knight-Lite's MERLIN went black and the four students left the classroom. There was no talking. No banter. They trudged down the hallway like doomed sailors following the sirens' call. Eventually they reached the outer doors to the vice principal's office and knelt in a line to await their punishment.

"Totally worth it," said Johnny.

CRIME AND PUNISHMENT

In which FangSwan does something scary in a cruel and . . . wait, did we do this chapter already?

The smooth, polished doors opened without being touched. Joey was the first to rise, and the four students entered with heads bowed respectfully, eyes to the floor. Carpets of different textures and thicknesses led across the spacious office. Fresh mountain air wafted in from three different windows.

Zato was seated facing away from them. His high-back chair was carved with a twisting dragon that formed the symbol for infinity—or the number eight, all depending on how you turned your head.

The chair spun and it was FangSwan who asked, "And *how* should I punish you?"

"Gah!" screamed Joey, while Johnny's dooley-bopper

went rigid with fright.

The ancient headmaster was a head shorter than Zato, making the chair slightly too big for him. A large chair can make a man appear comical. Not so with FangSwan. He did not look like too small a man, but rather too large a spider.

Peoni looked at him through a numb, frightened haze. When she spoke her voice seemed weak, as though her words didn't want to approach him. "Wuh . . . Why are you in Master Zato's office, Headmaster?"

"This is *my* office," FangSwan said. "*My* school. Every office, every room, every closet, every locker, every nook, every cranny. *Mine.*" His smile showed too many teeth. "I am here, because it pleases me to stay informed on the intentions of my enemies," he added.

"But Zato isn't your enemy, Headmaster," Joey said.

"Isn't he?" The silence following those words grew like a slow-creeping ivy. Sweaty eons passed before FangSwan spoke again. "But perhaps you are right. Let us return to the matter of your punishment."

"Nice one, Joey," Johnny said.

The walls around FangSwan were littered with

targets for incoming messages. As vice principal, Zato was responsible for much of the in-school communication, so missiles of all sorts periodically flew through his open windows. He had hung bull's-eyes to intercept these, made from different types of wood. Since every teacher had their own preferred method of message delivery, Zato could tell who had written simply by the sound their note made striking the target. FangSwan's target was made of old, heavy wood darkened with char. Sensei Renbow's target had a fresh note pinned to it with an elegant silver throwing quill. Peoni studied the loopy writing on the note, picking out choice phrases such as "vandals of good taste" and "the bloody heart of Theater was torn asunder." She rolled her eyes.

"Girl, Flim-Flam, Jalopy," FangSwan snapped. "Where's your pet?"

Knight-Lite wasn't quite sure how bad this was, but

he had settled on: *very.* In such situations, past experience had taught him to be as invisible as possible. FangSwan didn't look like the type of man to tie somebody up; he didn't even look like he'd bother burying the bodies. So when FangSwan rose to approach him, the sidekick let out a startled *meep.*

"H-here, sir," Knight-Lite said.

"Show me your chatty bracelet," FangSwan said. "I hear it knows things. Like a little talking library on your wrist."

Knight-Lite mutely lifted his arm up to the old man. FangSwan bowed his head to stare closely at MERLIN.

"Chatty bracelet, search for a complete list of Fang-Swan's blood enemies."

The red, blue, and green lines of light surged between the seams of MERLIN's metal surface as its electronic brain cycled up.

"COMPUTING," said MERLIN. "37,215 RESULTS FOUND."

The headmaster smiled again. Knight-Lite tried to smile back, but his mouth wasn't cooperating. "Good," said FangSwan. "Add the word 'living' to your search."

"ZERO RESULTS FOUND."

"Do we understand each other?" FangSwan said. MERLIN went black and a moment later activated its shield mode. The clackety whirl somehow sounded timid and unsure. FangSwan might have been talking to MERLIN, but he stared directly into Knight-Lite's eyes. Knight-Lite could not bring himself to meet the headmaster's gaze, but he could feel it like a spiked iron ball balanced on his head.

"Y-yes, sir."

"Excellent." The headmaster's hand was suddenly less than an inch from Johnny's eye, thumb and forefinger pressed tightly together. "What do you see here, Jalopy?"

Without hesitation Johnny said, "Nothing at all, sir."

"Exactly," said FangSwan. "What you can no longer see is a single grain of rice upon which I painted the face of my beloved mother, using a hair from the head of a hummingbird."

WISEMAN NOTE: Hummingbirds don't have hair, but the students smartly chose not to speak up.

FangSwan continued, "It is a thing of beauty that will reduce you to tears. That grain of rice was then fed to a chipmunk. That chipmunk was then released into the forest. You must find it and return to me so that I may extract the rice before the sacred image of my mother is lost forever."

Joey raised a hand and mistook FangSwan's stare of incredulity for acknowledgment.

"How are you going to get the rice back?"

"You are not ready for that information," FangSwan informed him.

"Okay . . . ," said Joey.

"You have until the beast relieves itself. That is your punishment."

"What's this about punishment?" came Zato's voice. He had returned from whatever errand he was on and quickly sized up the situation. Zato sounded

a touch uneasy. Of course, that's a perfectly normal reaction for anyone finding FangSwan in his office.

"Ah, welcome, Headmaster. I did not know you were visiting. I'll make tea."

"No. I am done here," FangSwan said. "Flim-Flam, Jalopy, Girl, take your pet and go. Do not return without that chipmunk. Tick, tick, tick."

Zato held the door for the four students, closed it behind them, and then turned to FangSwan.

"I'm sorry, Headmaster, just getting up to speed," he said. "Would you like me to acquire a chipmunk or have you already released it into the forest?"

FangSwan looked distracted as he returned to Zato's chair, and then looked up into his vice principal's unseeing eyes.

"What chipmunk?"

DOES A CHIPMUNK POOP IN THE WOODS?

In which Peoni is the unfortunate witness to explosive deforestation.

Joey, Johnny, Knight-Lite, and Peoni, unbeknownst to one another, all held the same embarrassing secret deep within them. It was a secret that only they, and perhaps an *extremely* talented wiseman with unprecedented access to the astral plane, could possibly know. It was something the four of them had had for as long as they could remember and they could not imagine that anyone else had one, too.

They each had theme music. It wasn't the *same* theme music, of course. Joey's was mostly guitar and drum. It sounded like imminent danger: *Da dum! da dum da dum da DUM! da DAAAAAAAAA!*

Peoni's was mostly string, with a lone cello, perhaps a trumpet far in back. *Daaaaa! Doo doo doo daaaaaaaaaa!*

Johnny's was a lot of piano and trumpet; he would have liked the 1920s. *Taa tingly ding DA tingly DOOOOO!*

Knight-Lite's music would have let you know the cavalry was on its way. *Doo DOOOOOO! dadada DOOOOOOOO!*

As they wandered the fields on the "quest" Fang-Swan had punished them with, they pulled out their theme music in a desperate attempt to make this an adventure.

"Johnny?" said Joey. "Did you just say 'taa tingly ding'?"

"Uh . . . no, Joey . . . no, I didn't."

WISEMAN NOTE: Yes, he did.

The quest was not going well. Peoni was perfectly capable of tracking and capturing a chipmunk, but a *specific* chipmunk wandering the great mountain wilds? Not being a wiseman, you might not know this about chipmunks, but *they all look exactly the same!* The only clue Peoni had to go on was that this was a chipmunk that had looked into the face of

FangSwan. So they were searching for a traumatized chipmunk.

"I'm telling you," she said to Joey, "those last eight all looked perfectly sane. We need to find a chipmunk that's really messed up."

"I think that last guy had a bit of the crazy eyes," said Knight-Lite.

"Nooo, he was just excited about a nut. I know the look," said Peoni.

"Well, maybe we should split up. Clinkety-Clank over here is scaring everything away," said Joey, nodding toward Knight-Lite.

"Okay, you three check the upper hills and I'll check out the bamboo forest," said Peoni, heading rapidly down the mountain on silent, bare feet.

"Why is Peoni going alone?!" shouted Knight-Lite, clomping over to Joey with bunnies and squirrels scattering in his wake.

If Peoni's feet were actually touching the ground, she showed no sign of it. The chipmunks of the area would later tell tales of a strange, half-liquid creature that spirited through the trees, snatching their people up just to give them a brief look in the eyes and move on. Clearly it was looking for the *chosen* chipmunk who would *change the world!* Poofykins, Eater of Many Nuts, was certain that *he* would be chosen. But he was put back down like all the rest.

Peoni rested for a moment at the top of a swaying bamboo stalk. She'd taken one semester of Languages of the Forest Animals and was trying to see what she could remember.

"*Chirp . . . chippety . . . squeak?* No, that's not right . . . uh . . . *squeak chippety?* Ugh, I don't know." She spied another chipmunk and swept down like a hawk, snatching it up.

"*Chirp chippety?*" she said to it.

WISEMAN NOTE: At this point your average goat-based wiseman would say, "Wha?" But I, being a superior kind of wiseman, am quite fluent in Chipmunk. I do not know what she meant to convey, but what Peoni actually said was: "<Meaningless Sound> nuts."

To which the chipmunk replied, "I'd like to go now, please, but if you have nuts I guess I'll take them."

Peoni tried again. "You are a bicycle! Ducks eat libraries?" Quite frankly, I'm impressed that chipmunks have a word for bicycle.

"Could I just go?" tried the chipmunk again. "There are guys in the forest doing strange things and I got stuff in my cheek pouches that I really gotta get rid of . . ."

Peoni understood "guys in forest," and she put the chipmunk down. He ran off muttering something about how foreigners should really learn to speak the language before they visit.

Knight-Lite meant well when he followed his three new friends along on the mission. After all, it was his fault for putting the show on in the first place. But Joey and Johnny would have had a better chance finding their chipmunk with a mariachi band following along. The knight-in-training just couldn't take a step without something clanking, clomping, or clinking. Even when his armor wasn't making a clatter, he was completely uncomfortable with the lack of conversation and kept asking questions.

"So what was the wiseman's riddle again?" he asked for the third time.

Joey intoned it again:

"You are not dead, shall soon awake
But listen well, do not mistake
A knight is close, and then goes far
Trapped inside, the up-down car

Three challenges shall come to thee
The first a duel, the next—can't see
The third a fight between two schools
To test his faith in honor and rules."

"Maybe the 'challenge' is not killing you for making me repeat it three times!"

"No . . . ," said Knight-Lite seriously. "The next three lines describe each of the three challenges. I mean, obviously the first part is about you in the astral plane, the second part is about me." Knight-Lite was excited. "I did tons of this stuff with Night-Knight. I think pretty much all his villains go for the riddling thing, particularly Post Note Pete."

Post Note Pete was one of the more conscientious criminals in Lemming Falls. If he wanted to rob a bank, he'd just leave a note about it on Night-Knight's refrigerator.

He was no master of poetry, but the bank robbery was thwarted and Knight-Lite was saved from an unpleasant cereal catastrophe.

"These things are always super clever and sneaky," said Johnny, remembering every episode of *The Pie and Ape Mystery Hour* he'd seen. "I bet the 'schools' are schools of fish! We're gonna fight *fish*!"

"We are *not* going to fight fish, Johnny!"

"Well, what about an octopus?" said Knight-Lite.

"That doesn't even make sense!" said Joey. "We're not gonna fight an octopus either!"

"Actually, I think we are," said Knight-Lite. He was floating fifteen feet in the air upside down, once again tied up from head to foot. But it wasn't with rope this time—it was by tentacles.

The chipmunk had been absolutely right. There were guys in the forest and they were up to strange things. Peoni perched in a thicket, watching them silently.

There were about thirty or forty Moonies in red and black, all wearing the Red Moon logo on their headbands. Some of them were unloading equipment from large crates while others were putting blinking metal devices on their arms, legs, and torsos. Four were hovering above the ground with jets of flame spewing from their complicated-looking boots. Another eight were dangling from tree limbs while guys below shot canisters of foam at their smoking legs.

Some of the activity was impressive in that way that only new technology can be. Most of it was just chaotic.

Peoni recognized Carl Crescent from the Red Moon billboards. He was pacing from group to group gesticulating wildly with his arms and dragging a harried-looking assistant around with him. "That's the stuff!" Carl would say in an excited voice, or "Great, fellas! Juuuuust great!" The fellow he said that to had his head stuck in what appeared to be a metal clamshell.

He sauntered over to a couple of kids fiddling with a palm-size device. When it made an angry buzzing sound, they dropped it and dove to the ground with their hands on their heads. It did absolutely nothing for several minutes until one of the brave souls poked it with a stick. The buzzing switched to a *flahshoorp* sound and the two Moonies were lifted into the air and sucked toward the device, where their heads met with a sickening crunch.

"HAHA!" said Carl, motioning for his assistant to make a tick on his clipboard. "You two really brought the shazzmo that time!"

Peoni had no idea what "shazzmo" was, and she couldn't understand why anyone would want some brought.

Two other Moonies were running in terror away from a trio of screaming darts that twisted and whirled through the forest after them. The Moony in the lead collapsed bonelessly to the ground as one of the darts caught him in the back. The second Moony took a dart to the shoulder and crumpled down on top of his buddy. They lay together in a sad pile, looking like an abandoned ninja sandwich.

"There we go!" shouted Carl, waving his hand at his assistant, who made another tick on the clipboard. "You really maxed the octane of that envelope!"

The third dart had not yet found a target, but a

promising flutter from the branches of a nearby tree piqued its interest. Three words bloomed in its tiny electronic brain: "movement," "girl," and "attack." As it grew closer to the movement's source, a hand snatched it from the air and smashed it to ruins against the trunk of the tree.

Peoni pocketed the remains of the dart and settled back into the depths of the tree to continue watching. The wayward dart was not missed, and Carl had already moved on to confer with a man standing by some crates. The figure was blocky and mostly lost in the shadows, but he didn't have the panicked movements of the Moonies, nor did he flail about theatrically like Carl Crescent.

The man stood still, looking quietly satisfied as Carl pointed out how great everything was going. When Carl was done the man pointed at the tree Peoni was hiding in and said something she couldn't hear.

"Aww, crackers!" said Peoni.

Do you know what you hear a lot when fighting a massive octopus?

"AAAAARRRGGGGH! Watch that tentacle!"

Joey had just screamed it for the forty-seventh time and they had been fighting the creature for only fifteen minutes. It had gotten to the point that Johnny didn't even really bother "watching that tentacle" anymore, because every time he did, some other tentacle that he hadn't been watching would bash him in the face. It was a bit like trying to wrestle eight joyful, bus-size puppies.

That didn't stop Knight-Lite from trying. "Golly!" he grunted with as much fury as he could summon. "You are such a jerk!"

Since his mouth was the only part of him that could still move, it really was the best he could muster. The octopus had a potent venom that it could deliver through needles in its suckers, and a healthy dose was currently making the rounds through Knight-Lite's bloodstream. You could track its progress by the quality of the young sidekick's insults.

"*Pants!* Yer a pair of lousy pants with . . . bad . . . pocket . . . holes . . ."

Joey's sword had been lost within seconds of the battle's start. It was quivering in a tree a hundred yards away. Johnny's hammer fared no better, and it landed halfway down the mountain. Dodging a tsunami of mountain octopus tentacles, Johnny held up his hand and shouted, "*To me, my hammer!*" But it didn't work, because Johnny's hammer can't do that.

So they punched the octopus.

A lot.

And the octopus didn't care. It was the only one

of them who still had a weapon. It had a firm grip on Knight-Lite's legs and was using him like an aluminum baseball bat. The baseball bat was still a little bit awake and continued to try to do his part.

"Yoooouu are . . . not good at . . . origami . . . I have a belly button!" And that was the last retort; the toxin had reached Knight-Lite's brain and he was out. Which was probably better for everyone.

Peoni was sprinting through the trees up the mountain. At her back, clumps of bamboo erupted into flames. A group of Moonies galloped in her wake, spraying random weaponry into the woods. She was less worried about herself than about the innocent trees that were getting needlessly wiped out. She somersaulted past a bright green stalk that evaporated in a shower of leaves as a ball of lightning struck it.

She landed, doing a neat A-plus roll, and sprang to a slender tree in the hopes of vaulting into the air. A lucky rocket strike snapped it in two just as she set her palms against its trunk, and Peoni plummeted to the ground. Her landing was strictly D minus.

It gave the Moonies a chance to catch up to her. They circled around and pointed devices that spun, beeped, and went *kachunk*. The biggest of the boys aimed a silver rod at Peoni. His name was Gordon, and this was going to be his moment.

Until recently, compliments were things that Gordon had only ever seen in blurry photographs. But since joining Red Moon, he had been congratulated for feats such as remembering his own name and finishing his lunch. Just minutes ago Carl Crescent had told him that he was the "Greatest Ninja Fighting Person. *Ever!*" and all Gordon had done was scratch his nose and discreetly adjust a wedgie. So at this moment his confidence had never been higher.

"Don't move or . . . I'll, uh . . . push this button right here," said Gordon as his finger trembled over a small green knob.

Peoni didn't move or even blink; she just looked at him. That was enough to make him squeeze the trigger.

Nothing happened. Well, not entirely nothing. The device sort of went *fleeerrrrrrrwhoop*.

The other Moonies began throwing helpful advice at him.

"Try shaking it!"

"No, you gotta smack it with your palm and then blow in the opening!"

"Tell it to fire, but make sure you pose it as a question!"

"Guys, she's running away . . ."

"Point the barrel at your head."

"That's not advice—she's actually running away..."

Peoni was bounding through the trees like a gazelle. The Moonies were back in pursuit like lions . . . well, no, not like lions, more like heavily armed ferrets. The explosions were coming fast and furious on all sides, and her theme song now had a full orchestra playing frantically in her head.

A dozen screaming darts had caught her scent and were nipping at her heels. They careened between bamboo stalks and ripped through foliage always just a few inches from the leaping, flipping girl. Peoni's energy reserves were depleting fast, and even her well-honed reflexes couldn't ward off so many attackers.

She blasted through trees in a curtain of flames, rolled down cliffs in a landslide of crumbling earth. Mud caked her face, rocket exhaust singed her hair, and the air crackled with electrical charges. Peoni lived for stealth; this was its polar opposite and in no way her idea of fun. As another homing dart detonated next to her, it occurred to Peoni that Joey would be having the time of his life. The thought gave her just enough strength to leap over the next ridge.

Joey caught sight of Peoni in midleap. She made an impressively action-packed silhouette against the

sun. He attempted to say hi to her, but by this time all three boys had various amounts of octo-venom running through them. So he actually said something poetic about an egg timer.

While Peoni had been spying on the Moonies, Joey and Johnny had been cleverly leading the octopus down the mountainside in hopes of retrieving their sword and hammer. It had been a good plan and the weapons had been recovered, only not by Joey or Johnny.

The octopus had a tentacle gripped around Johnny's hammer, another holding Joey's sword, and was flailing Knight-Lite around in a third. Knight-Lite was still completely out, so he was unaware that he had just been used to slap Johnny against the cliff face. That left five tentacles in reserve for Peoni, who landed directly in the path of the writhing nightmare.

She flipped over Johnny's hammer, ducked under Joey's sword, and twisted to avoid Knight-Lite's whole body. His plume breezed by her face, tickling her nose.

It was simply the worst moment for a sneeze. By the time she'd reached the "atchoo" part, the octopus had her by the leg. It held her down while lifting Joey's katana high overhead. It didn't exactly know how to use a sword, but Joey kept the blade so sharp it didn't really need to. Peoni waited for the inevitable end when a cavalry of motion-seeking rockets finally zeroed in on her—and found the octopus instead.

The octopus roared in angry surprise as a dozen needle-tipped missiles sank into the tentacle that was attempting to gift-wrap Peoni. Its grip loosened, allowing her to squirm free. Rejoining a badly winded Johnny, they each snagged one of Knight-Lite's boots and pulled him down to the ground. Johnny wobbled to their side, mumbling words that made little sense. Whether it was due to the venom, the cliff, or just Johnny being Johnny, nobody could really tell.

Between the four of them, they possessed enough combined strength to take on a midsize trembling autumn leaf. A maple leaf in any season would have clobbered them right now. The octopus looked as if he'd just returned from a bracing massage and a bit of therapeutic acupuncture.

And that's when Gordon figured out how to fire his silver tube. A beam pounded the tiger-striped octopus with a blazing blue light. The beast roared and spun to face the Moonies. As far as Peoni could tell Gordon had just fired an "Octopus-Angering Ray" and it worked brilliantly.

"AAAAARRRGGGGH! Watch that tentacle!" a Moony shouted.

The three ninjas and their ward made use of the distraction and disappeared into the woods, leaving the octopus to its play date with the Red Moons. Johnny would've laughed, but things seemed less funny on account of all the pain he was in.

As the least injured member of their party, Peoni took it upon herself to start hauling the unconscious

Knight-Lite back to school. Johnny followed, offering to take turns, and Joey limped after them both. He passed his hand through the space where the hilt of his katana should've been. He stopped and turned his head toward the distant sounds of slaughter and breaking equipment.

"This isn't over, octopus!"

FRESH MOUNTAIN AIR

In which the hills are alive with screaming.

Knight-Lite and Peoni were recovering in the KFA hospital. They were both stable, but the nurse suggested it might be some time before the octopus venom worked its way out of their systems. Joey and Johnny themselves had been laid out like doormats for two days the last time they got dosed.

Their sidekick was the hardest hit, but they had all had a taste of the toxin. At first it seemed that Peoni had been spared, but that was only because she had come late to the party. Soon she was trying to catch "all the pretty little fairies because they're sooooooo beautiful" and then she was facedown on the forest floor, snoring in the dirt. Joey and Johnny fared slightly better, and they managed to drag their companions back on crude stretchers.

Vice Principal Zato was the first person Joey and Johnny sought out once they recovered.

"I understand," Zato said seriously.

"You've got to believe us," Joey said.

"Yeah, there's a giant purple poisonous octopus hiding up in the mountains. And now he's teamed up with the Moonies and is supplying them with weapons taken from space aliens who want to steal our breakfasts. Also, he took our weapons and turned Knight-Lite into a baseball bat and he threw a horse at me that had train wheels for legs and a gramophone for a head. I'm really concerned about that horse! I mean, where does the steam come from?"

"Johnny, you are not helping," Joey said. "Ignore him, Master Zato, I think he saw those things, but I'm almost sure not all of them happened."

"So you saw this giant octopus too?" Zato asked. Joey was aware that his next words were being weighed and judged.

"... Yes?"

"Well, it's very dangerous. You should probably steer clear of it in the future." The vice principal leaned back in his chair and steepled his fingers in front of his mouth. "Tell me more about Red Moon Clan."

"Peoni knows more than we do, sir—she recovered one of the weapons they were using," Joey said, handing

Zato the remains of the dart Peoni had collected. "She also mumbled something about a 'man dressed in shadows' and a 'foppish clown' who had a dog that wrote on a clipboard. Once again, sir, the venom."

Zato examined the dart closely and said, "Come with me."

The heavy doors to FangSwan's office were as large and imposing as ever. Joey and Johnny stood out in the hall and stared at the crudely carved swan and its lone tooth.

Johnny nudged Joey, who was lost in a dark cloud of his own thoughts. "Do you think the headmaster will ask about Knight-Lite's bathroom habits? I haven't seen him go even once!"

"He spends a lot of time tied to a chair. I'm betting his fancy costume takes care of that," replied Joey.

Johnny's face shifted expressions as he struggled to decide if the idea disgusted him, or if he wanted a costume like that too.

Inside they could hear the muffled sounds of Vice Principal Zato's even tones followed by the headmaster's hissing reply. One moment FangSwan sounded sickly sweet, the next he'd switch to cold and mocking, and then he became threateningly abrasive. It was almost as if there were half a dozen FangSwans speaking with Zato, but when the doors finally opened only a single headmaster stood behind the battered desk.

"Johnny. Joey," he said in greeting.

"Headmaster, you got our names right!" Joey said.

"No," FangSwan intoned. "I didn't."

"Oh," both boys said sadly.

Remembering himself, Joey bowed respectfully before saying, "Headmaster, first I must humbly inform you that we could not locate the chipmunk. I am so sorry."

"What chipmunk?" FangSwan asked. "Zato, why is everyone so obsessed with chipmunks?"

Zato quickly stepped in. "Boys, please tell the headmaster what you told me and please skip the part about the horse."

Johnny muttered, "If you ask me, that's the most important part. . . ."

Joey filled the headmaster in on every detail he could clearly remember while Zato wove a convincing argument about being prepared for whatever Red Moon Clan might be planning. He handed over the dart and suggested arranging a meeting with Carl Crescent to discuss and . . . well, basically do what every civilized nation does whenever it thinks someone else is being sneaky. You dust off your biggest smiles and pull out your heartiest handshakes while your minions take a peek behind your "buddy's" back.

FangSwan actually listened to everything Zato had to say, but this was probably because he had never heard the words "diplomacy," "tact," or "mutually beneficial" before and was trying to understand them in context.

"That," FangSwan said, "was a lot of words. Now let me tell you what we shall do." FangSwan began to slowly pace across his office, his hands folded behind his back.

"Nothing," he continued. "We at Kick Foot Academy would have to dig a pit and stand in it to even look them in the face. As the great white shark takes no notice of the slimy banana slug, neither shall we concern ourselves with these . . . *henchmen*."

As he spoke FangSwan remained surprisingly calm. Only the last word held a touch of his usual disdain. His stroll had taken him to the entrance to his balcony. He slid his fingers between the sliding paper panels and eased the door open to the brisk morning air.

"They cannot truly harm the name of ninjaaaAAAAAAAAAAAAAAAAAAAAAAAAA!"

Joey and Johnny ran to where the headmaster stood screaming (arguably the single bravest thing either of them would ever do) to see what had caused it.

The view that currently burned in the embers of FangSwan's gaze was an enormous billboard anchored to the cliffs above the school, featuring the smiling face of Flippy the Ninja. His tubelike arm waved as he declared, "NINJA TIME IS FUN TIME AT RED MOON!" Just below Flippy was a photo of Carl Crescent leaning into the frame. His hand was cupped next to his mouth as he told the viewer via word balloon: "Now accepting transfer students from other ninja schools. You don't need a KICK in the FOOT to know who's got the best NINJA-MOJO. Act now! I'll see you at RED MOON!"

Joey and Johnny backed quietly away from the spot where their headmaster still stood, screaming at the monstrosity before him.

Johnny leaned his head in to Joey and said, "When do you think he's going to stop?"

"When he's done," replied Joey.

THE CHALLENGE

In which the bad guys
get their own chapter.

"**W**ow! That is *amazing*!" Carl Crescent said.

He ran his finger along the shaft of the black arrow that was currently pinning his assistant to the wall by the back of his uniform. The assistant, Leonard, hung like a terrified, mewling kitten in a Christmas stocking. The motivational poster taped to the wall next to him (one of many) mocked him with the phrase "Hang in there baby." The cat in the poster seemed to be handling its predicament with more dignity.

Red Moon Clan's offices were located in downtown Lemming Falls. The otherwise-drab building featured an animated Flippy the Ninja performing

somersaults in neon light across its roof. Carl peered through the window, scanning the nearby rooftops for any sign of anything.

"I mean, look at that shot! We're on the seventy-third floor. That is a bulletproof window! IM-possible!" he said. Carl ran the path between the small hole in the security glass to the still-whimpering Leonard. He made L-shapes with his hands as if he was framing shots for a major motion picture.

"Not impossible. Just exceptionally difficult," a shadowy figure stated from the cool depths of an intimidating chair.

The chair was designed to make a statement. It said, "*This* is a bad-guy chair. The man who sits here is a *bad* guy." It was made from the skins of several endangered animals, one of whom was known as the South American Raspberry Rabbit, named so due to the distinctive "*Thb-tb-tb-tb-tb-tb*" sound it made when it sensed danger. Through some trick of craftsmanship, helped along by the air trapped in its plush cushions, the long-gone rabbit continued to warn of danger every time someone sat down.

The shadow man knew this and always made a point of being seated before anyone entered the room. He didn't wish to give himself away and, well, he didn't want people to attribute the sound to something *else*.

"What does it mean?" Carl asked.

"A challenge," the shadow man answered.

"From who?" It was a question that answered itself, but Carl asked it anyway. The dark-red iron arrowhead, the ebony shaft, the fletching made of black swan feathers—this was an arrow shot from FangSwan's own bow. Fired by FangSwan. It was a rare honor to gain his personal attention. History showed most people didn't keep that honor for long.

"Red Moon is going to face off against Kick Foot Academy."

"*Ninjariffic!*" Carl said, and then thought about what the shadow man had actually said. "Er . . . I mean, are you sure that's a good idea, sir? After all, they're *real* ninjas."

"Things are going according to plan," said the shadow man. "This arrow is a clear sign. This arrow is a testimony of how far FangSwan has been pushed. This arrow is on fire, by the way."

It was true. The wall and, to a lesser degree, Leonard, were both smoldering. Carl extinguished the problem with his thirty-two-ounce BigSlurp cinnamon twist Americano with a chaser of goat milk. Leonard yelped in pain, proof that Carl's coffee had not been perfect sipping temperature.

"Thanks, Lenny. Why don't you take five," Carl said. Leonard made motions to leave, but, still being pinned to the wall, he did not make it very far.

Carl Crescent turned back to the shadow man. "But seriously, sir. We'll never survive a war with KFA."

"Ninjas do not go to war; that's what armies do. When ninja clans disagree they solve their problems with a challenge. There will be set rules, and time to prepare. Traditionally it is the Test of Three, to be held on the next solstice or equinox," said the shadow man. "And FangSwan is nothing if not traditional."

In the bad old days, a ninja clan usually discovered that another clan had a problem with them when they woke up dead, or at least in possession of a lot less blood than they had gone to bed with. Technically a

challenge had been made, but the time between issuing the challenge and actually taking part in it was
much, much shorter. Often measured by the swing of a
katana, or the flight of an arrow.

Of course, the bodies did tend to pile up, leaving
nothing resolved. There was always a lone survivor
who would grow strong with a head full of revenge, and
the process would start all over again.

Ninjas used to have very large families. It's not that
they wanted them. It was just insurance: the theory
was, if you had enough kids, one of them was *bound* to
be the Chosen One.

It worked until the ninja world began getting over-
run with Chosen Ones seeking vengeance for one thing
or another. It was making it hard to get stuff done, and
finally everyone agreed to set some ground rules.

"We will meet his challenge," the shadow man said.
"And win or lose, I still win."

He began to laugh. A low chuckle that slowly filled
the room as its mocking sound grew louder—an unat-
tended teapot of laughter bubbling over and making a
real mess of the stove with its evil spilled water. Carl
Crescent joined in, his own laughter serving as a higher,
happier chorus to accompany the shadow man's mirth.

The shadow man stopped suddenly. "Why are you
laughing?"

Carl didn't really have an answer on the tip of his

tongue. "Um . . . it was funny?" he tried. No, that wasn't right, so he tried again. "Show of solidarity?"

"Well, don't," the shadow man said. "You don't get to laugh. I'm laughing alone on this one."

Carl replied by shutting up, allowing the shadow man's laughter to bubble forth anew. It started and stopped, not really gaining back the momentum it had achieved the first go-around, and eventually ground to a halt altogether. He pivoted in the chair to stare at Carl, the shadows in his face clearly annoyed.

"No, the moment's over. Thanks a lot, Carl."

LETTERS FROM TING

In which Ting is charming and pathetic.

Hi, guys and Peoni,

Sorry to leave so suddenly, but I had to go and it was never going to be a good time, so I did what I thought would be best. I hope you're not too mad.

I like it here, but Headmaster would be furious (I'm not supposed to use his name). Nothing is up to his standards, but then again—nothing ever is. My time at KFA obviously served me well. I know I had some troubles there, but I've been doing really well at Red Moon. I haven't been to the hospital once since I got here!

Yesterday I attended a class and I was the only one who put my mask on properly. After class the teacher told me I had unlocked an achievement (?). Also, we were sparring and one of the older boys asked me to take it easy. ME?!

HA! (NOT REALLY!)

Your friend (pleeeeeeasse forgive me),
TING
ninja cadet-in-training
p.s. Extra sorries to Peoni.
p.p.s. At lunch, food is served on plates!

THE FOOD SITS HERE
UNTIL YOU EAT IT!

Hi, guys and Peoni,

WOW! Big week! I'm finally getting used to sleeping in a bed. I didn't realize how much the wind blowing through my mulberry bush helped me drift off.

Class-wise I'm doing great! You're not going to believe it, but I'm at the top of my martial arts class for the second week in a row. Today our coach had us take turns on a balance beam and we hit each other with padded sticks until some- one fell into a kiddie pool filled with water. At the end of class I was the only one still dry!

Remember the time we did the same thing with Sensei Kendu? Only it was a high wire, and it was on fire, and we used pole arms? And instead of kiddie pools she had a pit filled with scorpions? And I still ended up wet.

Anyway, check it out! I got a promotion (see below). My teachers say that I've got what it takes to go all the way, and it's only another $29.99 to advance to the next level.

Your friend,

TING

ninja

p.s. Is Peoni still mad?

Hi, guys and Peoni,

Tell Peoni that I got her letter. Very funny. Disappearing ink written on flash paper. Ha, ha, ha (in case you can't tell,

that's sarcastic laughter). I'll just say that it's a lucky thing that I shave my head. Does this mean she forgives me?

I heard about the headmaster's "challenge." It could've been cool, but it sounds like it's gonna be a big stress monster. I mean, we're going to be taking part in the Test of Three. It's like we're hobbits or something. I'd like to say Red Moon stands a chance, but you know we don't.

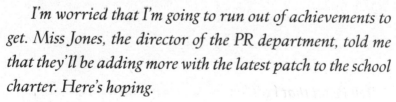

Moving on to the GOOD news! I got promoted again!

More good news. I've unlocked thirty-seven out of fifty achievements. Most of them are not that hard; the real trick is thinking to try them in the first place. I got one yesterday for doing three flips in a row.

I didn't really land the third one, but they gave it to me anyway.

I'm worried that I'm going to run out of achievements to get. Miss Jones, the director of the PR department, told me that they'll be adding more with the latest patch to the school charter. Here's hoping.

Your friend,

TING

ninja master

p.s. Tell Knight-Lite he can never replace me! I'm a ninja MASTER. :)

Hi, guys and Peoni,

Cool! I didn't know Knight-Lite knew Night-Knight, but I guess it makes sense. I've been a big Night-Knight fan since I was a kid! I have an action figure of him back home.

BOX ME!

They've started training me to use some weird stuff. I can't really talk about it, but they called it super-ninja gear. Personally, it doesn't feel very "ninja" to me, but my immediate supervisor said that I had to "think outside the box." Still, it does some pretty cool stuff, when it works.

HA! I sound like Headmaster saying something isn't ninja enough.

Your friend,

TING

ninja master–sergeant at arms

p.s. No one could do Headmaster's voice like you, Johnny. I miss you guys.

Hi, guys and Peoni,

Okay, things are weird here. Recently Red Moon has started accepting a lot more students. The halls are getting crowded with other kids . . . and not-kids. Many of these new guys are adults! And you should see their drawings of Flippy! They're terrible! Not sure what's going on, but it feels like this place has seriously lowered its standards.

Someone from marketing (Betty?) told me they want to use my story in their next round of advertising for Red Moon. All about my time at KFA and the "meteoric rise" I've had with Red Moon Clan. I pointed out that meteors actually fall and then either burn up or hit the ground and explode. She just laughed and called me a "smarty."

I guess it's kind of an honor, but I get cold sweats thinking about what Headmaster would think.

Your friend,

TING

ninja master–sergeant at arms–guardian of the north wind

p.s. Thank Knight-Lite for sending me the autographed picture of Night-Knight.

Hi, guys and Peoni,

I just got back from a meeting with my guidance counselor. I tried to talk to him about changing the location of our training grounds. Sometimes I think we're doing things to directly antagonize Headmaster. I had a long talk, with examples, about how that is a really bad idea. I mean really, really bad. But no one wants to listen. They act like ignoring Headmaster is an option. Sure . . . I guess you can ignore a volcano, too—UNTIL IT EXPLODES!

I can't stop thinking of that golden-feathered osprey that dove down, captured, and ate one of Headmaster's fish from the koi pond. The next day the lunch ladies were slinging osprey hash at us, and we all got golden writing quills (mine had a little maroon splatter on it—ew). And Headmaster hated those fish!

Here's hoping SOMEONE listens to reason.

Your friend,

TING

ninja master-sergeant at arms–guardian of the north wind–tamer of dragons

p.s. I said no about using my life story.

Hi, guys and Peoni (and Knight-Lite, too . . . I guess),

NO. NO. NOOOOOOO! Do not tell FangSw— . . . *Headmaster about anything! EVER! I don't want to be collateral damage if or when he snaps.*

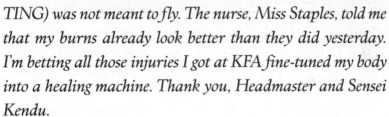

In other news, I DID finally wind up in the nurse's office.

Can't reveal much about what happened, so let's just say that man (or at least TING) was not meant to fly. The nurse, Miss Staples, told me that my burns already look better than they did yesterday. I'm betting all those injuries I got at KFA fine-tuned my body into a healing machine. Thank you, Headmaster and Sensei Kendu.

Your friend,

TING

ninja master–sergeant at arms–guardian of the north wind–tamer of dragons–air walker

p.s. Ask Knight-Lite if the word "ScarTech" means anything to him.

Hi, guys and Peoni and Knight-Lite,

I got all seventy-five achievements today! The final achievement was for using all the water fountains in the building. Lucky thing I get thirsty all the time, but seriously, who would even think to do that? There was a little ceremony and I got to meet with Carl Crescent himself!

He appeared right in front of me with a poof of smoke (but I'm pretty sure I saw him hiding behind the curtain when I walked into his office—didn't say anything, though). Still, it was really cool, like in the commercial.

He's taller than you'd think and he's got perfect teeth. He said I was the first person to ever unlock all the achievements. They're making a seventy-sixth achievement for getting all the achievements and they're naming it after me! He called me their best and brightest!

It was a really good day.

Your friend,

TING

ninja master–sergeant at arms–guardian of the north wind–tamer of dragons–air walker–guru of the unfindable

p.s. Tell Peoni that Mr. Crescent's got nothing on her stealth skills. The smoke pellets are cool, though.

p.p.s. The Test of Three thing is coming up soon. It kinda sucks that our schools are fighting, but at least I might get a chance to see you guys.

Hi, guys and Peoni,

Hope you get this! Strange stuff is afoot at Red Moon. I know the Test of Three is coming up and I've got a bad feeling about it.

Yesterday the third floor was labeled off-limits. Normally

I wouldn't have bothered to investigate, but the closer we get to the Challenge the more secretive all the teachers seem to get, and I had to know why.

I tried to sneak in and take a look, but I'm no Peoni. Some upperclassmen stopped me—that is, until they got a look at my face. Once they saw it was me they let me do whatever I wanted. Guys . . . I know this is hard to believe, but over here, I am a total kick-butt, whirlwind, shark-bite ninja. Some of the other students are a little afraid of me. I'm the BRAD of the Moonies!

I KNOW! And if you're laughing . . . I hate you.

Anyway, there were a ton of giant crates inside one of the third-floor gyms. The same kind of ScarTech crates a lot of our other special equipment has been shipped in, but these were big. Like, CAR big! BUS big!

Never found out what was in them, though. I heard a door close, some footsteps, and then there was smoke. POOF. Suddenly Carl Crescent was there. He asked me a bunch of stuff. It felt like a test, and it felt like I failed. But then he asked me if I was ready for the Challenge and that Red Moon was proud to have someone with my skill at "Ninja Fu" (it's "ninjutsu," right?). Carl seemed really distracted and was halfway across the room before he even remembered to throw one of his smoke pellets to cover his exit.

Today a lot of the top students were getting pulled out of class for "special training." I wasn't picked, but I think that's because I used to go to KFA. I'm certain it has something to do with both the Test of Three and those crates.

Maybe it's nothing, and I know I'm betraying Red Moon by telling you . . . but you haven't seen what some of the stuff they give us can do. Those crates scare me, and I . . . I thought you guys should know.

Your friend,

TING

ninja master-sergeant at arms-guardian of the north wind-tamer of dragons-air walker- guru of the unfindable-rear admiral of the western fleet

p.s. "Rear admiral"? Now I know they're just making stuff up.

SHARP AND POINTY

In which we are almost 100 percent certain
that the boys will probably, definitely
not make it any further. Perhaps Ting
can carry the rest of the story!

Peoni stood next to Knight-Lite, looking around the classroom nervously. It was exactly the right class to be nervous in. Sharp and Pointy dealt exclusively with the avoidance of all things that could slice, dice, and poke. The walls were adorned with daggers, sickles, and animal tusks. Hanging from the ceiling

were chains holding shark teeth and rusty farm equipment. They swung ominously in the breeze coming through the open window. Your daily grade was tallied by how many bandages you used by the end of class. It was hard to stand in that room and not feel like a peach in a blender.

"Where did you say they went?" Peoni asked Knight-Lite again.

"I don't know, Peoni. They were gone by the time the morning arrow woke me up!"

"You caught the morning arrow?" Peoni asked, turning to Knight-Lite in surprise.

"Oh! No. Johnny drew my head on a block of wood and left it next to me. It was the *thunk* that woke me up!"

FangSwan had done his very best to ensure that there were few to no relaxing moments for the students at his school. Lazy Sunday afternoons had been eradicated and hammocks were considered contraband. Ninjas were always alert and prepared to look death in the eye. So it was very important to him that even sleeping had an element of danger. But how?

In a blinding moment of joy the headmaster had placed the archery field directly facing the student sleeping quarters. This ensured that no students of his would ever awake with a song in their heart. An arrow, maybe, but never a song.

"Here comes the professor," Peoni said. She had been hoping Joey and Johnny would walk in before the teacher, but it was too late.

Dagger McJones didn't look anything like a ninja. He wore a grubby green jacket with the collar flipped up and a Windsor cap pulled low over his head. The parts of his face that weren't covered in shadow were craggy, and every wrinkle had a scar to keep it company. When he moved he made a soft clanking sound, as though hundreds of metal things were buried in the folds of his clothing.

"'Allo, ya buncha twits!" he said as he walked in. He smacked one of the hanging strings of teeth, sending it crashing into a chandelier of railroad spikes. Soon the room was clanging danger-ously and jaggedly. "How's abou' I throw some knives a' somma yew?"

Dagger McJones opened every class with this offer.

He made it sound like that was the best deal you were going to get all day, but he never got any volunteers.

"Guess ah'll jus havta pick one-a yew blighters; ow's abou' . . ."

Peoni caught sight of Joey and Johnny wobbling toward the door to the class-

room. They were covered in round sucker marks and looked as though they were having a small argument on the correct operation of a doorknob.

"Oh no," she whispered to Knight-Lite, "they've been at the octopus again!"

Joey was trying to open the door by mashing his face against the window. One of Johnny's toes had successfully entered the room, but try as he might, no other parts of him were getting under that door.

Peoni waved her hand to get the teacher's attention. "Professor," she said loudly, "could you please tell us how you got that scar on your face?"

A bright smile bloomed on Dagger's face. He looked like a man who'd been asked to show pictures of his children. "Well, i' was quite a story, luv! This bloke I was playin' pool wit', he sez I bet you twenny quid yew can't take a bot'le to tha face, an' then I sez . . ."

The man was lost in happy memories and failed to

notice Joey and Johnny's shambling entrance into the classroom. Brad took notice and then glanced at Peoni's pleading face. He quickly bumped into a table, causing the coils of barbed wire on top of it to jangle. It created just enough noise to mask the sound of the door shutting behind the tardy ninjas. Peoni flitted to her friends' side, ushering them to a place behind a group of taller students. Brad snuck over to help.

"Hello, cuckoo clock," said Joey, looking with a dazed expression at Peoni. With a suspicious glance at Brad, he asked, "Are we at surfing class?"

"You two came to Sharp and Pointy class filled to bursting with octo-venom?" she whispered at them. "You're gonna use up all the Band-Aids!"

"Iz not over yet, Occopus!" mumbled Joey.

"These guys were fighting a purple tiger mountain octopus?" said Brad, impressed. "How are they still standing?"

Johnny was batting at a collection of coyote teeth hanging from twine. Peoni pulled him away. "This is the absolute worst place for you two to be right now! Just try to stay quiet!"

McJones hadn't even noticed Peoni slinking away. He was positively riveted to his own story. It must have been getting to the good part, because his accent got thicker and no one could understand a word. "So's I tellz this Jack-o-ninny, yew go' abou' one minu'e afore I—"

"What happened to that man's *t*'s?!" Johnny's voice

was loud enough to make the cutlery rattle.

"Gah!" said Peoni.

"Ooooh," said Brad.

"Wha' you say?" said Dagger McJones.

Johnny stalked across the room, his hands held out to grasp the professor by his shoulders. Dagger instantly put a hand under his grubby coat. "Don't worry!" Johnny said with great compassion. "We're gonna help you find your *t*'s!"

"Are you off your bleedin 'ead?!" said Dagger.

"Joey! Now his *h*'s are gone! There's an alphabet thief afoot, and he has stolen letters from this poor man!"

Joey wrestled the shoe off a confused student and held it aloft for all to see. "I think I found one of his missing *h*'s!!!"

"*Yay,*" said Johnny, turning back to the professor and handing him the shoe. "Now you can say 'h-h-head' properly!"

"Ladies 'n' gents, looks like ah've go' a coupla volun'eers."

"I never saw so many knives come out of one coat before!" said Knight-Lite as he peeled the backing off another bandage and stuck it to Joey's nose.

Peoni was doing the same to Johnny. Both boys were lying on their backs on a patch of grass, softly groaning. They each had enough bandages to make them look like a four-year-old's sticker album. It had been a couple of hours and the octo-venom seemed to be wearing off.

"It would have been worse if Brad hadn't been there," said Peoni.

Joey groaned at this. He groaned even louder when he saw Brad was right in front of him, looking concerned.

"I didn't do much, really," Brad said.

Brad had managed to keep the professor's knives from skewering the two boys by subtly yanking them around by their belts. The puppet show was so convincing that Joey and Johnny looked as if they had been dodging intentionally. They might have even escaped completely unscathed if they hadn't insisted on ending the performance with an elaborate bow that sent them careening into the porcupine pen.

Joey groggily pushed himself up onto an elbow, the other hand holding his head. "Ugh."

Peoni put a palm to his forehead. "Would you puh-lease give up on the octopus! You can get another sword and hammer!"

"What!" shouted Johnny. He got his face so close to Peoni that his dooley-bopper smacked the top of her head with each word. "Hammers like Mr. Thumpsworth do *not* grow on trees!"

"They do when they're made out of wood!" Peoni shouted back.

"He was taunting us with our own weapons, Peoni! That walking calamari is going down!" Joey said.

"Purple tiger octopi are tough adversaries," Brad offered. "Since brute force isn't working, have you tried tickling?"

"A ticklish octopus?" Johnny asked.

"Yeah," Brad said. "They're practically made out of armpits."

Joey just growled and tried to steer the conversation in another direction. "Any word about the dart Peoni snagged?" he said to Knight-Lite.

"Actually, yes! It's definitely ScarTech. It's basically a cheap rip-off of the same technology many of Lemming Falls' superheroes use. Night-Knight says you find it in the hands of a lot of low-level supervillains."

"So can you do some sort of fiddly-thing and make it not work so good?" Joey said in his very best technobabble.

"I think I can, but I'll need supplies. KFA doesn't have techy stuff, but if we can get some more Moony gear . . . just bits and pieces."

"They may not be the brightest," said Peoni, "but the shadow guy isn't going to let us get that close again. Plus, we don't have the time to go searching the mountains for them."

Joey smiled. "Oh, we don't have to go searching. I know right where we can get you all the parts you need."

Peoni looked at Joey, puzzled, and then she figured it out. "Nooooo, Joey!"

"It's not over yet, octopus. . . ."

AN UNWELCOMED
WELCOMING

In which Headmaster FangSwan is forced
to look up the word "hospitality."

Three helicopters appeared over Kick Foot Academy, drawing a crowd of curious onlookers. Ninjas knew what helicopters were, but the vehicles seemed out of place over the quiet mountain school. A monstrous eagle or a winged samurai demon would have fit the surroundings better. Yet there they were, buzzing KFA's rooftops, their rotor blades roaring rhythmically thumping thunder.

The whirling birds flew in perfect formation until they centered themselves over the KFA training arena. The hand-built amphitheater was the only space large enough for them to safely touch down.

But they didn't bother to land. The rear door opened up on the central helicopter. With a blast of recorded guitar rock, a dozen Moonies made bold swan dives into the open air. Each student was tethered to a bungee cord that pulled taut moments *after* the students smacked into the ground in a series of sickening thuds. The bungee cords jerked the now-unconscious students back up into the air, where they bobbed like an amateur puppet show. The song continued rocking out, telling the listener that "only the best survive when the eagle fights the lion with lightning power!"

The Kick Foots watching from below tried to be polite about the spectacle, oohing and aahing at appropriate intervals. When it became clear that maybe dragging unconscious people across gravel with a helicopter wasn't the intention of the show, Peoni, FuShoe, and Joey mercifully cut the groaning students free.

The other two helicopters conferred for a moment before lifting upward another thirty feet. Their passengers made a less impressive but altogether safer descent to the arena floor. A few of the Moonies kissed the ground after disconnecting themselves from their bungees. The prerecorded anthem still blasted out the copter's speakers, but now it just seemed sad.

One Moony, a sort of foreman, had been busy directing his brethren to first clear the wounded and

then deal with the crates that had also been unloaded. As the helicopters departed he learned that his own bungee had never been detached. He reflexively grabbed onto a low wall at the edge of the arena, but that just made it worse. The cord pulled taut, and then with a *twoing* he vanished into the open sky.

Red Moon Clan had arrived for the Test of Three.

The amphitheater filled with students in red and black. The Red Moons brandished their blinking, beeping weapons, while the Kick Foots flashed their swords and throwing stars. Every dirty glance felt like a lit match near dynamite.

The teachers from both schools conferred on the

observation platform, chatting politely over cups of tea.

Johnny spotted Ting among the sea of red and ran over. Joyfully lifting him off the ground in a bear hug, he shouted, "Look, it's TING!" Joey and Peoni grabbed Knight-Lite by his arms and pulled him through the crowd to introduce him to their old friend.

"I hear you're quite the ladies' man," Peoni said to Ting.

"I-I . . . Oh, shut up," Ting said, hugging her hello. It was unsettling to see him standing there in his Red Moon costume. It was even more unsettling that the costume suited him. He looked at home in his skin, confident, but he also looked worried. "You don't think Headmaster saw that Red Moon ad, do you?"

"You're still alive, aren't you?" Joey pointed out.

A flock of birds was released to a collective gasp from the crowd. They wheeled about in circles across the schoolyard, scattering when the crackle of fireworks exploded from all sides. Two attractive young women in spangly costumes and two men in black body stockings danced through the throng. The men held aloft an eighteen-foot-tall puppet of Flippy the Ninja, who appeared to backflip over everyone's heads as the men twisted hidden control rods. The sparkly women threw out handfuls of candy, which the Moonies eagerly scrambled for.

Two Red Moon students, one small, the other large and doughy, stepped out in front of the teachers' observation platform. The smaller Moony grabbed a microphone from the backpack speaker system the larger one carried. When he spoke, his voice came out deep and booming.

"The Lion of the South. The Dragon of the West. The Yeti of the North. And the Giant Anime Manga Robot Warrior of the East."

His arm pointed in each direction as he spoke— down, left, up, and right. Having completed the circuit once, he repeated the gestures with increased speed. Again. And again, until his arm spun in a continuous circle.

"You know him! You love him! Red Moon Clan Lemming Falls' regional branch manager! *Caaaaarrlllll Crescent!*"

A series of smoke puffs began on the far side of the circle and rapidly tore across the arena one after the other, like the tromping footsteps of an invisible giant. They advanced toward the stage, faster and faster, until they culminated in an explosive cloud of black smoke and fire. A hidden fan buzzed to life, blowing the cloud away to reveal Carl Crescent. His arms were raised in greeting and his sash blew dramatically in the fake wind.

He gestured toward the glittery young ladies, who

positioned themselves at his elbows. Flippy, under the command of his puppeteers, did a series of backflips behind him.

The Moonies roared their approval.

When the clamor eventually died down, Vice Principal Zato made his own entrance. He walked up to the stage using his cane to tap out a path.

"By way of introduction," Zato said, "the headmaster has asked me to read you these four words." He pulled a small scroll from his robes and, sliding his fingers across its surface, read the message to the gathered crowd.

"I am behind you."

Screams of horror greeted this announcement as every single member of the audience spun around as one. Arms were raised in defense, and panicked Moonies activated weapons that hummed and sparked to life.

But FangSwan was not behind *everyone*. He couldn't be . . .

(Right? Why don't you check just to make sure.)

Zato had been speaking to only one member of the audience. He turned his blind eyes toward Carl Crescent, the only person who hadn't bothered to turn around.

A woman screamed and the two sparkling beauties ran in opposite directions. Flippy crumpled into a lifeless pile of fabric as one of the puppeteers fainted from shock. The microphone hit the ground and squeaked awkwardly before going dead. Carl himself finally turned and yelped, falling backward off the platform and to land sprawling in the dust.

There, in the spot Carl had been standing in, was the small, elderly headmaster.

"Welcome," FangSwan said, "to Kick Foot Academy."

Later, behind closed doors, the traditions were honored. FangSwan made tea for his guests and served them without speaking. He made no comments about the entourage who sat with Carl Crescent, nor about the fact that he was required to make tea for them all, and that this forced him to reheat the small kettle several times. Silence loomed as he went about the business of stirring and pouring.

After being served his cup of hot ginseng tea, Carl almost asked if he could have a mocha latte instead. Something in FangSwan's body language suggested that he would humbly murder Carl if he spoke, so Carl kept quiet and drank his tea.

"Excellent," Zato said in an upbeat tone. "With the tea ceremony completed, let us now air the nature of this disagreement." He swept his hand toward Fang-Swan. "Headmaster, would you like to begin?"

"They are not *ninja*," he declared.

"Of course we are," Carl said. "Didn't you see our pajamas? They're *nintastic*."

The cup FangSwan had been holding exploded into shards. Hot tea dribbled between his fingers and onto the floor.

"Is it the technology?" Carl asked.

"It is the everything," FangSwan said. "But yes. The beeping and the booping are a part. Ninjas do not have jet packs or laser-guided missiles."

"Well, *our* ninjas do," Carl said. "When the first ninja crawled out of the sea, wasn't the katana a cutting-edge piece of technology? Those proto-ninjas didn't insist on using weapons that had been made by monkeys seven hundred years ago, did they? No! They got their hands on the best weapons they could find."

This is what Carl Crescent had been chosen for: his ability to monologue. Also for his relative ignorance of FangSwan. Carl was not a brave man, and if he knew even a sliver of FangSwan's history he wouldn't have been nearly so calm. He wouldn't even have been on this mountain. But Carl was lost in his own words now. He might as well have been talking before an adoring, live studio audience.

"That's what I do for them! While *you* hold them back with techniques and tools that belong in a museum, *I'm* busy supplying the ninjas of tomorrow with the technology of today!"

The shards of broken pottery in FangSwan's hands exploded into a fine porcelain dust.

Carl turned to his assistant. "Music soars

triumphantly, zoom in on my face, cut, and post," he instructed. "Splice Flippy dance number four at the end. Maybe show a Kick Foot ninja and dub in a sad trombone. Lenny, I want to see that go viral by ten, okay?"

Lenny gave his boss a wide smile and double thumbs-up. There was a *ba-loop* sound and the assistant tucked his smartphone back into his sleeve.

Carl turned back to FangSwan. "No hard feelings, Fangsy. If you want we can do another take. You can even spin it your way, so your people can put it on a scroll, or a cave painting, or whatever."

The molecular bonds holding the dust together in FangSwan's hands broke apart, allowing it to dissipate into its component atoms. Tradition stated that no harm must befall his "guest." Flossing was also tradition, but sometimes you forgot and just went to bed. Did the world end? No. No, it did not.

Zato stood up and walked between the two men. "So, can it be agreed that the dispute is over the use of modern technology?"

It was agreed. The dispute was over technology.

Next, the nature of the Test of Three needed to be addressed. They took turns choosing the three challenges. Carl declared a duel of champions. FangSwan chose a demonstration of stealth. The final test was traditionally a battle royal, and both men readily agreed.

Finally, the terms of victory and loss.

"Red Moon Regional Branch Manager Crescent, as the Challenged you get to declare your victory conditions first," Zato stated.

"Simple," Carl said. He pulled a piece of paper out of his collar and read from it. "When we win, I will have the total dissolution of Kick Foot Academy. Additionally, FangSwan shall have the title of 'Headmaster' stripped from him in perpetuity."

Zato stood up, knocking his chair back. "Y-you cannot mean . . . certainly tradition states a reprimand, a-and acquiescence to certain . . ."

"Oh, I can." Carl smiled. "And I do. My lawyers hired translators. And my translators hired historians. Together they went over the scrolls, and every other thing you haven't bothered to upload to the internet. It is within my rights, and I will have it. It's going to be NINTACULAR!"

For the first time since setting foot on the Kick Foot campus, Carl Crescent seemed dangerous.

Zato drew breath to continue the argument but stopped at an unfamiliar sound behind him. Few sounds were unfamiliar to the blind swordsman, and he was not prepared for it. It was rich and warm, the sound of a wise grandfather watching a new puppy wrestling with an oversize bone. It was honest laughter and it was coming from FangSwan.

It was the most disturbing thing Zato had ever heard.

THE DUEL OF CHAMPIONS
In which you may feel free to cry;
there is no shame in it.

"**B**raaaaaaad!" cried Joey, shaking his fist at the sky.

Joey had just been signing up for his chance to be the chosen champion. It was a delicate operation, since the parchment tacked up to an ancient stone pillar was already black with signatures. He'd found a tiny patch of white at the paper's edge, and if he squeezed it in sideways his name might just fit. . . .

FangSwan walked out onto his balcony high above where Joey was crouched. "It's Brad," said the headmaster. "You are all wasting your time. It's always been Brad. It will always be Brad. Brad is the champion." FangSwan then turned and returned to his office, slamming the door. The *J* and *O* were still drying under Joey's pen tip.

"Seriously, did you expect anything different?" Peoni asked. She looked down at Joey, who was still crouched at the parchment, his pen dripping black ink on his black shoes. "He's Brad."

"He is really good," Knight-Lite said. "His hair blows in the wind even when there isn't any wind!"

"Yeah," said Johnny. "And he always has mints and he offers them to you just when you want one."

"But he does it in such a way that you don't feel like it's because you have bad breath," added Peoni.

"And his teeth are white, but not creepy white," said Knight-Lite.

"He's pretty much better than us at everything," said Johnny. "It'd be weird if FangSwan chose you."

"Oh, I'm sorry," said Joey, glaring at his friends. "I must be at the wrong sign-in sheet. This is clearly the one for the weekly Brad Lovefest. Where's the one for the champions?"

"Get over it," Peoni said. "What if Headmaster had chosen me, instead? Would you have stood here growling, '*Peoni*'?" She did her best Joey impersonation, and by "best" I mean not very good.

"Maybe," Joey grumbled, but he didn't mean it.

"And anyway," said Johnny, "if anybody ever writes a book about us it won't be the *Adventures of Brad*! He'll just be a bit part. They'll call it *Johnny and Joey, NINJA FRIENDS!*"

"*PEONI THE NINJA and Her Friends Johnny and Joey,*" said Peoni.

"*With Special Guest Star Knight-Lite,*" said Knight-Lite hopefully.

"*FUSHOE THE AMAZING NINJA!*" shouted FuShoe as she passed by.

WISEMAN NOTE: Wrong, wrong, wrong, and wrong. FuShoe would eventually get a book of her own, but it would be titled *FuShoe: Freelance Dragon Veterinarian.*

"It's probably for the best," Peoni said, pulling Joey to his feet. "You *still* haven't gotten your sword back from that octopus."

Johnny brightened. "Last time was sort of fun! I'm pretty sure he likes us now. I named him Mr. Squiddles."

They weren't friends, but the purple tiger mountain octopus had grown to recognize the two ninjas. It is even possible to say it had grown fond of their frequent encounters. For a variety of reasons, it normally met someone only once. Joey and Johnny were becoming part of its daily routine: wake up, brush your beak, squibble and schloorp about, beat the holy stuffing out of two ninjas, retire with a good book. So, no, they weren't friends—a friend rarely uproots a tree with its tentacles and uses it to try to knock your head into your stomach—but it did *like* Joey and Johnny. It liked Joey and Johnny the way a dog likes its favorite chew toy.

Whatever their relationship, Joey and Johnny continued to trek up the mountain every day. They had not (yet) managed to retrieve their sword and hammer, but they did gather plenty of broken pieces of Moony ScarTech. More than enough for Knight-Lite. Also noticeable was the reduced level of octo-venom coursing through their veins after each encounter. Either Joey and Johnny were getting better at dodging tentacles, or the octopus was taking it easy on them. The last time the boys made it down the mountain they were hardly even slurring their words.

"I think he likes being tickled," Johnny said.

"Maybe," Joey said, not wanting to admit that it was Brad who suggested the tickling in the first place.

"Is that all you're going to say?" Peoni asked. "'Maybe'?"

"Maybe," Joey said, with just a hint of a smile.

While the others talked, Knight-Lite found a table and began tinkering with the various technical bits and pieces Joey and Johnny had gathered for him. He snipped wires, bolted bolts, and fused things together with a pocket-size laser. On his wrist, MERLIN suddenly pulsed and beeped.

"Um, guys. The first challenge is beginning."

The training arena of Kick Foot Academy was the largest single structure at the school. It was a circular slab of rock so enormous that more than half of it hung over empty air. Live trees anchored to the side of the mountain helped support it from below, and a waist-high wall ran along its outside curve to discourage, but not entirely prevent, students from taking the quick way down.

Its surface was made of marble hand-laid in a simple concentric pattern. In the center stone was a small handprint so finely detailed you could make out the wrinkles and folds of the skin. It was placed there on the last day of the school's construction, when Fang-Swan knelt in the middle of his arena and, with a sound of thunder, struck the stone with his open palm. It was his signature for a finished work of art.

Students from both schools were gathered in a half circle, separated from one another by a raised observation platform where the teachers stood. Carl Crescent was standing close to FangSwan and taking sips from a paper cup. Every so often he bobbed his head toward the headmaster and tried to make a comment about the day. At one point he even handed FangSwan a steaming paper cup of his own. The curl of steam disappeared the moment the cup touched the old man's fingertips, but Carl never noticed. FangSwan did not take a sip.

Zato addressed the assembly, his quiet voice helped along by the curved walls of the arena. "The first test is a duel of champions; the winner will be the last man standing. If there is any confusion to the outcome for any of the challenges, an impartial judge will have final say in the matter." He gestured to a figure in stiff blue

and white robes wearing a large woven basket on its head. The basket marked it as an Empty Monk.

Empty Monks dedicate their lives to becoming entirely void of all thought or opinion. By becoming empty vessels, they hope to better receive the wisdom of the universe. This makes them highly prized and respected as impartial judges.

WISEMAN NOTE: Fine! Yes! They are excellent observers, but they still look like twit-brained fools with those baskets on their heads. It's no better than Dillydale Fwops and his bucket.

"Kick Foot Academy, present your champion," said Zato.

A puff of smoke flashed in the center of the arena, and Brad appeared. He bowed to the headmasters.

"How'd he do that?" Carl said under his breath.

Brad was dressed in black with a dark amber sash. A yin-yang symbol decorated the left side of his chest, and on his head he wore a gift from Knight-Lite. It was a black superhero mask that fit his face as if it had been

painted on. The mask stopped just below his hairline, allowing his blond locks to blow majestically in the wind. (It was a windless day.)

WISEMAN NOTE: I want to be able to do that with my beard! I still can't figure out how he does it. There's something different about that boy. . . .

From the sideline Peoni nudged Joey and whispered, "Admit it, he looks like a champion."

"I'll admit nothing," said Joey, "but he gets bravery points for wearing a superhero mask in front of Fang-Swan." Poking Knight-Lite, he said, "Guess we know who your favorite is."

"Wha . . . I . . . uh, no!" stammered Knight-Lite.

"Guys, the Red Moon champion is coming out!" cried Johnny.

The Moonies began to chant, stamping their feet in unison as a bulky figure emerged from a rain of sparks and orange fog. The arena filled with a vibrating hum that shook pebbles loose from the surrounding walls as he approached. The champion looked tall and hulking and was apparently wielding every weapon and device the Moonies ever built. A puttering engine was strapped to his back, belching a blue cloud of exhaust.

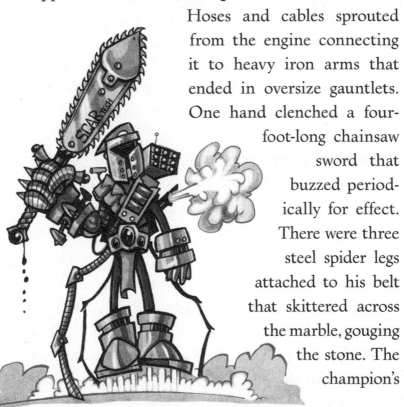

Hoses and cables sprouted from the engine connecting it to heavy iron arms that ended in oversize gauntlets. One hand clenched a four-foot-long chainsaw sword that buzzed periodically for effect. There were three steel spider legs attached to his belt that skittered across the marble, gouging the stone. The champion's own legs dangled above the earth, clad in hover boots that hummed and stirred up swirls of dust. The monstrosity came to a halt three feet from where Brad stood motionless. Steam hissed and metal parts shifted, clicking into place.

The thing lifted a heavy hand to its welded-iron face mask. Six-inch spikes popped from its knuckles, making the head behind the mask yelp in surprise. There was an awkward pause as the champion tried to figure out how to get the spikes to retract. When the right toggle was found he reached once more for the face mask, only to have the spikes pop out again. "Just a moment . . . ," came a muffled voice. There was another long pause, a click, and with a hiss of escaping steam the iron mask lifted on small hydraulic arms.

The face underneath was red, sweaty, and streaked with oil.

Peoni clutched Joey's arm as she gasped, "It's *Ting!* The Red Moon champion is Ting!" Word spread from Kick Foot to Kick Foot as the whole crowd's collective jaw dropped open. Brad and Ting were going to fight. In the shocked silence that followed, only Johnny had something to say.

"Way to go, Ting!" he cheered.

"Why is he doing this? Didn't Ting wet himself once to get out of sparring with Brad?" Peoni asked.

"Oh golly, you don't want to do that when you're

wearing that many electronics," Knight-Lite said. "Night-Knight once defeated the Winged Weasel because he had to wee in the middle of a fight. The Weasel suit wasn't designed for that and started smoking, then flew into a wall. Later the Weasel admitted the worst part was landing upside down."

"Knight-Lite," Joey said. "Shush."

"A lot of electrolytes in pee," Knight-Lite continued. "Increases conductivity."

Ting heard none of this as he stared, panicked, into Brad's calm face.

"Nice to see you, Ting," Brad said. "Sorry we have to fight."

Ting looked at Brad pleadingly. "I don't know what any of this stuff does!" Target lasers swiveled, speckling Brad in little red dots. A chamber popped open from Ting's back, revealing an array of missiles. Blades sprang from the sides of his arms and his spider legs scrabbled at the ground aggressively. Three soda-can-size pods rolled out from a bandolier across his chest. They bounced as they hit the ground at Brad's feet and unfolded into small turrets that swiveled to target his head.

Brad pulled a pair of dark wood nunchucks from his sash. He gave Ting a reassuring wink and said, "I'm going to do everything in my power not to hurt you, Ting."

"Thank you so much!" Ting gasped. Unfortunately

his words were lost to the sound of twelve missiles shooting from the open bay at his shoulder. They collided at the point where Brad had *been*, distorting the air with a ball of fire. The ninja was already twenty feet away, his chucks moving so quickly the audience could feel the wind. The soda-can turrets struggled to track him, launching a series of exploding pellets with a *pom pom pom* sound. They made an impressive display and did a fair amount of damage to the arena, but they failed to connect with their target.

The same could not be said for Brad. He struck the ground with the spinning chuck, knocking all three turrets off their tiny feet. Two of them exploded as they fired their payloads directly into the ground. The remaining turret loosed its grenades into the sky, where they lit the clouds orange.

The only voice that could cut through the sounds of battle was the theater-hardened cry of Sensei Renbow. "Good job, Brad!" he said.

Brad rolled across the marble and sprang up next to Ting. The missile bay continued to fire, but Brad managed to rip it away before he or Ting could be injured.

Unless he was somehow controlling the devices with terror, it seemed unlikely that Ting had anything to do with these attacks. He just looked deeply sorry to be involved. His eyes widened in surprise as his chainsaw sword roared to life. Soon he was wrestling with his own arm as it tried to swing the sword at Brad.

Both champions were bathed in a shower of white sparks as Brad caught the sword's spinning teeth with the chain from his nunchuck. He held the blade just inches from his neck. Rocket engines on Ting's arm ignited, pushing Brad to his knees. Joey saw something he'd never seen before: a look of strain on Brad's face. He guiltily swallowed the momentary pang of satisfaction he felt.

Ting shouted over the buzzing whine of the chain sword, "I'm not doing any of this, Brad! I can't stop it!"

"No . . . ," Brad grunted, "no need to apologize, buddy, I got this handled...." He wrapped the nunchuck chain tight around the sword's blade and somersaulted, twisting the blade in a corkscrew motion that snapped the huge gauntlet off Ting's skinny arm. Ting waved his freed arm in victory and began slapping at the harness across his chest, trying to unbuckle himself.

The chain sword hit the ground, skittering toward the arena's outer edge. Brad was dragged along behind it. The rocket engine continued to roar, spitting flame at the side of Brad's face and arm. He released his nunchucks, letting the whole spinning, flaming mess hit the low wall at the edge of the arena and careen into the open air down below. He allowed himself one brief second to lie on the cool marble, then he rolled back to his feet.

Ting was poking at the belt around his waist. Its buckle pulsed a bright purple. "I don't know what this means!" he shouted as Brad ran toward him. The rhythm of the pulsing sped up and was accompanied by the rising whine of a tiny motor revving out of control. The light was flashing as fast as a hummingbird's heartbeat by the time Brad slashed at the belt, freeing Ting. Ting wanted to help but Brad pushed hard against his chest. Still wearing his hover boots, Ting was propelled across the marble like an air-hockey puck, flying to the opposite side of the arena, where he slid into the arms of his friends, who had moved to catch him. Turning back, he saw Brad holding

the belt above his head, a shadow against the now-continuous blazing-hot glare. Brad said, "Don't worry, I'll save—"

Then the white-violet light ate the champion's silhouette until there was nothing left.

Brad was gone.

HIDE AND SEEK
AND SPANK

In which Peoni shines invisibly.

None of the Kick Foot students were excited about the test of stealth, least of all Peoni, who was their chosen champion. There had been no time to get over the loss of Brad. He was supposed to have been immortal. His defeat at the hands of Ting made Kick Foot Academy's victory no longer certain.

The Moonies, on the other hand, had begun to strut. After throwing a victory party for a very reluctant Ting, Carl Crescent debuted a video celebrating his school's epic triumph. The video highlighted the valiant warrior Ting crushing Brad in single-handed combat. Carl memorialized the defeated Kick Foot champion and expressed his regret that Ting was unable to save Brad from his own fatal mistake. The final image of the film was a tasteful photo of Brad above the words "Died With Honor," and then, *ka-chunk!*, a rubber stamp pounded the word "DEFEATED" on his face in red letters. No one had seen or heard from Ting since the video was released.

"Yeah, but Brad's not dead, right?" said Joey. Peoni had no answer for him, and Knight-Lite just teared up again.

Johnny answered the question confidently. "No, he's Brad!"

Joey wanted to take some comfort in that, but he knew that Johnny had said the same thing about his goldfish, Mr. Bubbles. He probably thought Brad was on vacation in the toilet too.

Desperate to change the subject, Peoni asked Knight-Lite about his progress on the antitechnology device.

"It's going okay," Knight-Lite said, wiping at his eyes. "If I had two more days—"

"You don't!" said Peoni. "You have *one* more day and we *need* it!"

"We won't if you get defeated by the Red Moon champion, too," said Johnny. "I bet we get tomorrow off if that happens."

"We'll get every day off *forever* if that happens!" said Joey, whacking Johnny's dooley-bopper.

"I'm not going to lose," said Peoni. "I can't bear to be in one of Carl's videos."

They were walking her down the hallway to the start of the test and past other Kick Foots. Many of them were staring at tear-stained photos of Brad, while some offered Peoni a wave and a word or two of encouragement.

FuShoe clapped her on the shoulder and said, "Give them a whiff of your feet, girl!"

"He's not going to see me or smell me, Fu," replied Peoni.

"Poke 'im in the eye with your hair, Peoni!" said Whistler, patting her head. "Aaahgh!" he screamed in mock agony, as if he'd petted a porcupine.

"Humph," said Peoni, smoothing her hair. "He will not be spurting blood, just tears of humiliation."

They arrived at the entrance to the library. The test would be conducted within its labyrinth of shelves and corridors. It was many floors deep and filled with dim, flickering candlelight and dark shadows—the perfect place for a game of hide-and-seek.

Carl Crescent stood on a small stage with a hand on the shoulder of his champion, a slender boy dressed in an outfit that was covered head to toe in hundreds of tiny plastic lenses. It made him look as though he'd just stepped out of a bubble bath. A pair of bug-eyed goggles covered his eyes. Carl smiled widely and raised an eyebrow at Peoni, who was dressed exactly as she had been the day before.

Peoni turned to her friends. "I wish I didn't have to go in front of everybody."

"That's what the school champion does," said Joey, giving her a nudge forward.

"I'm the champion of *stealth*!" she hissed back. "Being seen is totally counterproductive!"

Zato gave an encouraging nod in Peoni's direction.

"Oh, great," said Peoni, "the blind guy saw me!" She tried to give FangSwan a humble look of gratitude for choosing her as the school's champion, but he took no notice of her. His eyes were fixed on the ground, his eyebrows indicating an elevated threat level.

"Why did FangSwan pick me? I don't think he likes girls. . . ."

"You're not a girl, Peoni," said Johnny, "you're a ninja!"

With that, Peoni walked to the stage, faced the

audience, and gave a confident wave, drawing cheers from the Kick Foots. Zato raised his arms to silence the crowd. "The rules are simple: Each champion will be given a piece of parchment and then they will enter the library. Your goal is to place your parchment on your opponent's back without being seen. Return here in thirty minutes and we will have our winner."

Carl handed his champion a crisp white envelope, which the boy opened and read. He gave Carl a nod and a confident thumbs-up as he tapped a button on the side of his goggles. He immediately shrieked and sank to his knees, croaking, "My eyes!"

Carl shook his head and sighed. "No, no, you have to wait until you're in the dark!" He motioned for the school nurse, who came and dragged the boy away.

Everyone shuffled their feet impatiently as they waited for a new Red Moon champion to be chosen. It had to be someone who fit in the bubble suit. Peoni was looking down at her feet, so she was unprepared for FangSwan's voice in her ear. He was closer than the minimum safe distance. "Peoni," he said, and handed her a small tube with a rolled-up scroll inside.

"Thank you, Headmaster," she said. She momentarily glowed with pride as she thought, He knows my name! Then she quailed in terror as she thought, He knows my name!

The new Red Moon champion, Steve, stepped up

to the stage, crisp white envelope in his hand. He was very careful not to touch the button on the side of the goggles. Zato tossed an ancient coin into the air and Steve called heads. He pumped his fist and winked at Peoni when the coin landed in Zato's palm heads up.

"The Red Moon champion has won the toss and will enter the library first," said Zato.

Steve walked past the open door of the library and turned around to look at Peoni. "Be seein' you," he said, touching a button on his glove. He tipped an imaginary hat at the audience, and his suit flickered as one by one the bubble lenses adopted the colors of his surroundings, until finally Steve disappeared altogether.

The audience gasped, "Whoa."

"We sell gloves like that in our Red Moon gift shop!" Carl proudly told the crowd. "Great for faking injuries that'll get you out of work!"

Peoni entered the library one minute later. She let her eyes adjust to the darkness and then unrolled

the parchment scroll. Two words were painted on it in
FangSwan's bold brushstrokes:

Tests of stealth rank just below televised sneezing contests as the worst-possible spectator event. No, wait.
Novel writing—an absolutely terrible spectator sport.
The whole point is, there's nothing to see. So tensions
were thick among the milling throng of Kick Foots and
Moonies. For thirty minutes the crowd of spectators
muttered quiet curses and anxiously toyed with their
weapons. Only the Empty Monk seemed unaffected.

Professor Dagger McJones kept putting his hand
under his coat to finger the bazillion knives he stored
there. He looked as if he wanted to start a fight, or fin-
ish a fight, or both. Sensei Kendu watched him closely,
and kept spinning her blades in her wingtips. She was
either warning him off, or telling him that she'd back
his play. It's really hard to read a bird.

Carl was busy with his assistant, filming an

on-location infomercial. ". . . and this ancient library, filled with moth-eaten scrolls, will be the future location of our spectacular Red Moon Warriors spa! Never again go into battle without a cinnamon scalp wrap!"

Cracks radiated out from where FangSwan's feet gripped the paving stones. A fuse that only the Kick Foot students could see had been lit in the ancient headmaster. They wanted to run, but they all knew running would do them no good. If FangSwan went off, he would take the whole mountain down with him.

So there was a tremendous collective sigh of relief when the library door opened. Steve came out alone, portions of his bubble suit winking on and off as he spun in a circle, searching the crowd, the ground, and the trees. He no longer looked smug. "Professor, she had to have cheated. There was no one in there but me!" He spun in another circle. "Plus, she didn't come out. That means I won!"

"How could I not have come out if I never went in?" asked Peoni, who was standing right by Steve's shoulder.

"Gah!" yelled Steve.

Zato smiled. "Will the champions please show their backs to the judges?"

Peoni turned around. There was nothing on her back.

Taped on Steve's back was a piece of parchment,

the words "KICK ME" painted in bold brushstrokes. Below that was another sheet of paper with a small Red Moon logo in the right-hand corner and the words "KICK ME" in stark block letters. Below that was a torn sheet of paper with the instruction "KICK ME HARD" handwritten in charcoal. A fourth sheet of paper featured an arrow pointing at Steve's butt.

There was a snicker from the audience as someone noticed the blinking lenses on Steve's bubble suit. Some of the lenses blinked on and off, while some of them remained permanently dark. There was a pattern to the dark lenses, and when his suit blinked on, it could be easily read: "HERE I AM!"

FINAL PREPARATIONS

In which we are introduced to a brand-new
character who is promptly forgotten.

"**T**oday, we won," FangSwan told the assembled Kick Foot students. "Hoo. Ray.

"I suppose this makes us even. Brad's been disintegrated, but one of the Moonies had some pieces of paper taped to his back." With his hands, he balanced invisible scales.

"Yes. It is balanced. The rules say so. Rules make us who we are. Even when they are twisted into an unrecognizable shape. Without rules, anything could happen. Anything." He spoke as if something he swallowed was trying to eat its way out of his throat.

"What are we?" he asked the dead-silent room. Students were suppressing their heartbeats in an effort to not be noticed. "Terrified" probably wasn't the answer he was looking for.

"What are we?" he asked again.

Joey took a deep breath. "Ninjas?" he offered hopefully.

"Are we?" The thoughts boiling through Fang-Swan's brain were huge and dark, and Joey had become their focal point. He felt his back strain and legs begin to buckle under the weight of those thoughts.

"Headmaster FangSwan," Johnny said. "W-we are ninjas." He grabbed Joey's arm, which helped both boys remain standing.

"Yes, we *are* ninjas." FangSwan smiled. "This makes tomorrow exciting! Some of you may have heard what is on the line. If we win tomorrow, those sad little clown men will no longer be able to use their tricks and toys. They will no longer taint the name of ninja." He paused to snatch a fly out of the air and held it in his fingertips, its wings still buzzing. He spoke to the fly now.

"If we lose, this school will be shut down. I will never again be a headmaster. Perhaps I will drive an ice-cream truck, selling delicious treats to all the happy boys and girls. Maybe I will join a team of Canadian lumberjacks. I have always enjoyed cutting things down." He turned again to his students. "But, in the long run, if we lose tomorrow it will mean only one thing."

He stared, saying nothing else. The silence grew

desperately uncomfortable and everyone looked at Joey, hoping he would fill it. He had spoken before; certainly it couldn't get any worse for him if he spoke again. Joey swallowed and asked the question he wasn't sure he wanted answered.

"What will it mean, Headmaster?"

"I," FangSwan said, "will be free . . . of rules." He released the fly and watched it flee through the window.

"We won't lose, Headmaster!" Johnny said, fist held high. There were some guttural affirmations from the other students. If FangSwan had had a heart, it might have been touched.

"What?" he said, waving his hand in the air as if shooing gnats. "Do what you want. Either way. It does not matter."

He pulled a scroll out from the depths of his robes. "Tomorrow we will need twenty participants for the Battle Royal. Here is my list: Aardvark, Pointy Knees, Uncle Monkey, Ugly Toes, Birdbath, Flagpole, Crouton, Fish Fingers, Spit Take, Squinty Bob, Underpants, Banjo, Doorstop, Stench-Foot, Crybaby, Bug Thumbs, the Honorable Lord Useless, Harpy, JimJim, and Bippity Bop."

As he spoke each name a student stepped forward and said a hurried "Thank you, Headmaster," before bowing their head. Joey and Johnny were the last to do this, and they added a discreet fist bump before lowering their heads like the others.

"Classes are dismissed for the rest of the day. I will not need any of you until tomorrow," the headmaster said as he walked toward the door. Before exiting, he turned to look over his shoulder. "Girl!" Peoni looked up at the old man, eyes wide. "Your performance today was . . . acceptable." With that, he left.

Peoni's victory party broke all the rules that ninjas live by. It was bright, loud, and untouched by the shadow of the morning's coming battle. They sang happy songs about stabbing things and opened their

mouths wide to catch the cakes and cookies hurled at their faces. The lunch ladies were true professionals when it came to throwing a party.

Peoni would probably have greatly enjoyed the celebration if she had not disappeared the moment she caught wind of it. Whistler and Spratt prepared to lead a small team to search for her, but Joey reminded them how fruitless that would be. "She's probably in the forest celebrating with the squirrels," he told them.

So FuShoe slapped two starfish to the sides of her head and gave a speech on Peoni's behalf. "Thank you all sooo much," she said while dancing to the side to avoid a bowl of seven-layer dip. "If you want to know how I did it, I just hung from the ceiling by my hair and ordered my chipmunk minions to do the dirty work." She used cupcake frosting to write the words "KICK ME" on the back of a pizza. "The hardest part was teaching the chipmunks to write!"

Knight-Lite came late to the party. He scanned the crowd with his shield deployed, unable to tell what was food and what was student. Johnny startled the sidekick when he erupted from a pile of jelly rolls. The loss of concentration left Knight-Lite vulnerable, and within minutes he was cocooned in crepe paper and hung from the ceiling. "Guys," he said, his voice muffled, "I have something to show you!"

Joey pulled him down and the three of them

scrambled out of the party to an empty courtyard outside.

"Where's Peoni?" asked Knight-Lite.

Joey started to answer, "She doesn't like parties..." when a shape dropped out of the tree above them.

"I like parties," said Peoni. "I just didn't want to have to give a speech." She had cake and frosting in her hair.

"You were at the party the whole time?" Johnny said, flicking at the bits of cake. "How...?"

"I just hung from the ceiling by my hair and had my chipmunk minions bring me cupcakes," she said. "FuShoe made a better speech than I would have."

They walked over to a bench next to an abstract sculpture of FangSwan punching a dragon in the face. Just before they could get to business, a short man in a dull gray suit walked up to them.

"I wanted to tell you," he said to Peoni, "you did a wonderful job today. I could not have been prouder." His voice had little inflection. His face, unmemorable.

"Who was that?" Joey asked when the man left. He sat down on the bench in the shadow of the dragon.

"I think he's our stealth teacher," Peoni said, but she didn't sound at all certain.

"Really? I had no idea," Johnny said. "Man, he's good."

"Who's good?" Knight-Lite asked.

"Never mind," said Joey, already forgetting the encounter. "Show us what you've got."

Knight-Lite produced two brass disks from his pocket. "This is it," he said excitedly. "Keep these up your sleeves. Tomorrow during the melee, put one in either hand and clap them together as hard as you can."

Joey rolled one of the disks over in his fingers. It was about the size of a pocket watch. One side was flat, while the other was rounded and fit nicely in the palm of his hand. Each disk had a red, shiny, very pushable button on it.

"And that's all I have to do?"

"Golly," Knight-Lite said. "I guess. It's got more than enough power. The Moony gear is pretty cut-rate stuff, but they don't lack for power. If it comes to stability, safety, subtlety, reliability, and precision—yeah, they suck. But not power. Especially not for a one-shot item like this."

"And you're sure it's not going to blow my arms off?" Joey asked.

"Almost totally certain," Knight-Lite said. "Just get in the middle of the Moonies before you activate it. I

Knight-Lite's **TechWrecker** Instruction Manual

Place disks in opposite hands. Make sure both hands are in easy reach of each other.

Clap hands together.

Resulting Electromagnetic Pulse destroys nearby tech.
(I have no idea how to draw this.)

Celebrate with preprepared victory dance.

have no idea what kind of range it'll have."

Joey took another long look at the two metal disks and their invitingly red buttons. Knight-Lite had even inscribed the word "PUSH" on them. He slipped one up each sleeve. "Good," Joey said. "Because I think I've got the wiseman's riddle figured out."

"Yeah?" said Johnny. He was perched on the back of the bench like a bizarre black bird.

Joey quoted, "'*The third a fight between two schools. To restore his faith in honor and rules.*'" He finished and gave his friends a significant stare. No one said anything.

"You all saw FangSwan today," Joey said.

"I didn't," Knight-Lite said.

Knight-Lite's **TechWrecker** Warnings and Advisories

Note: TechWrecker is not a toy. For emergency use only.
Note: TechWrecker is designed for a single activation. Use and discard.

WARNING:
There is a very small chance of accidental sundering of one (17%) or more (12%) limbs after successful activation of the TechWrecker.

Joey explained, slightly annoyed. "The headmaster was on the edge! One step away from killing everyone on this mountain, and not a big leaping stride, either. A teeny, tiny baby step."

"Oh, I don't know," said Johnny. "He was talking about becoming an ice-cream man."

"And then he'd kill us all with ice cream!"

"That would work. I'm lactose intolerant," Knight-Lite said.

Johnny pondered a moment. "I hope he kills me with Mint Mountain Chunk."

Peoni looked surprised. "But you don't like Mint Mountain Chunk."

"I know," Johnny said. "I wouldn't want to be killed by a flavor I loved. It might create negative associations later."

Joey sighed. "The point is, we *need* to win tomorrow. Not just to beat the Moonies. Not just for the school. But to save our lives and FangSwan's sanity."

WISEMAN NOTE: It was debatable how much sanity FangSwan had left to save. Just don't have that debate when he's within earshot.

"So we're in the melee tomorrow, right, 'JimJim'?" Johnny asked.

"You got it, 'Bippity Bop.'"

"*And* it's crucial that we save the school?"

"Right again."

"So tomorrow, we'll need to be at our absolute best," Johnny said. "We'll want every advantage we can get, right?"

Peoni rolled her eyes. "Oh, you cannot be serious."

Joey ignored her. "The proper equipment, a good night's sleep, a decent breakfast . . ."

". . . our favorite weapons?" Johnny finished.

"You read my mind, Johnny."

Peoni stood with her arms extended, palms out flat. "Guys, no," she said. "Please, be reasonable."

"Reasonable people don't go to school to become ninjas," Johnny declared.

Johnny put his hands out with interlaced fingers. Joey stepped up and Johnny flipped him high into the air. Joey landed on the nose of the dragon sculpture and pointed his finger at the mountain.

"You heard that?" he said. "This ends tonight, octopus!"

BATTLE ROYAL

In which the boys make falling
off a cliff look difficult.

The sun rose on the morning of the great battle and three arrows thunked harmlessly into the wall of Joey and Johnny's empty room. Nerves had woken Knight-Lite up early and he was already busy defending himself from breakfast. Joey and Johnny had never come home.

"Where are they?" Peoni whispered to Knight-Lite as she pulled a bagel laden with cream cheese out of the air. She looked at it still spinning on her finger but had no interest in eating.

"I don't know," Knight-Lite said, wiping strudel off his face, "but I have a pretty good guess." Peoni groaned and set her captive bagel free, watching it join a flock of

hurtling donuts. They sat quietly together while breakfast enveloped them.

As they headed to the arena with the rest of the
students, Peoni scanned the top of the crowd, hoping
to see Johnny's dooley-bopper. Almost everyone was
there, but it was Vice Principal Zato's nervous pacing
that crushed Peoni's hopes. Zato was a man who didn't
waste movement, the calm in the storm; to see him so
obviously upset was . . . upsetting. Occasionally Zato
would pause to say something to FangSwan, but if the
old headmaster heard him he showed no sign of it. He
just stood perfectly still, his white robes softly glowing
in the morning sun.

In contrast to the creepy stillness of FangSwan, Carl
Crescent was a blur of movement. He tapped his expensive shoes on the dirt of the arena, sending up little dust
clouds that threatened the white perfection of Fang-
Swan's robes. He scribbled furious tick marks on his
clipboard, pausing occasionally to touch a hand to his
earpiece. He had the look of a rock star setting up before
a big show. It had obviously been a late night, for he
was on his third mochaccino double espresso triple-
sweetened with a shot of lychee juice. It had left him
with a fusion of excitement, trepidation, and focus.

Puffs of smoke were blooming periodically from his
collar and armpit, making him look like a malfunctioning android. A fellow Kick Foot told Peoni that it

had been happening all morning. It seemed that the regional branch manager was so distracted that he had set off one of his trademark smoke pellets *before* pulling it out of his pocket.

Just to the side of the two headmasters, the basket-headed Empty Monk waited in a serene state of observant nonself. Toward the back of the platform, Senseis Kendu, McJones, Renbow, and the rest of KFA's teachers stood in rigid anticipation of the day's events. Even Sensei Ohm managed to look as rigid as it was possible for a floating ball of light to look.

The Battle Royal was about to begin.

The KFA champions took to the field. The students moved into formation on the east side of the arena facing the headmaster. Joey loves dramatic timing, Peoni thought, and desperately hoped that this was his dumb idea to make things tenser. More "ninja."

"There are only eighteen KFA champions," Carl Crescent said. "I think we have grounds for a forfeit."

"Congratulations," FangSwan said. "You did not even take off your socks."

There was a brief discussion of the number of students, but the rules did not require a full twenty participants in the melee. The rules must have also declared no substitutions, because neither FangSwan nor Zato called for volunteers.

FangSwan walked in front of his gathered students

and said nothing. He just looked each and every student in the eye for three seconds.

All things considered, it was one of his better speeches.

The time had come for Red Moon to take the stage. Carl dusted himself off and stood before the gathered crowd of students and teachers. The kid with the speakers on his back jogged out and handed Carl the mic. With a splash of his previous showmanship he posed dramatically, looking left and right to take in everyone assembled. He wore the face of a fortune-teller predicting important but disturbing news.

"This test is coming to a close, and with our victory today, so too will this school come to a close." He gestured sympathetically toward the Kick Foot students. "Does that mean all of you are no longer ninjas?" He waited three beats and then allowed a magnanimous smile to bloom across his face like a smoke bomb.

"No! Because I have a special offer for you. Red Moon Clan will be accepting any student from the Kick Foot Academy into our ranks. If you act immediately we'll even waive the 'draw Flippy' requirement and give you half a semester's credit to honor what you have already learned here. This may be the end of Kick Foot Academy, but it doesn't have to be the end of your ninja career. Thank you, RED MOON!"

Carl looked up in thought for a moment and then

raised his hands as if to hold back angry questions. There were none, but Carl had a script and refused to deviate from it.

"Now wait a minute, wait a minute. Some of you might miss your old school, but you don't have to worry. Red Moon plans on buying this property and using it as our corporate retreat. So stick with Red Moon, climb the company ladder, and you can schedule a visit to your old stomping ground once a quarter. And while you're here you can take part in some exciting trust- and team-building exercises to help you focus on making Red Moon—and yourself—the best you can be!"

A low thrumming shook the mountain, forcing Carl to raise his voice. The shakes resolved into rhythmic thuds that grew steadily closer. "Ladies, gentlemen, bird-women, sentient balls of light—without further ado, I give you the future of ninja . . . MECHA-MOONS!"

A fifteen-foot banner unfurled in a shower of sparks, displaying the Red Moon logo. Rocks and earth bounced in time to the metallic thuds, which grew still louder and closer. A bulge appeared in the center of the logo, growing and growing until a metal fist burst through. An army of robots marched through the tattered remains of the banner, moving purposefully toward the arena. The two hapless Moonies who had been holding the banner were dragged along behind.

The rest of the students, Red Moon and Kick Foot alike, hurried out of their way.

The robots were tall and hulking. Some were roughly human-shaped, while others looked like walking construction equipment. Some rolled out on treads or skittered like bugs on spindly legs. A robot whose lower body spun like a top was having a difficult time getting past a decorative stone lion, so it pulverized the statue with a swipe of its massive arm.

FangSwan bent his head toward Carl Crescent. "My grandfather carved that lion with his false teeth," he said as though pointing out a pleasant place to take a photo. "I'm going to make you chew me a new one."

"Haha!" said Carl through his clenched, perfect

teeth. His smile never wavered, but the comment made his eyeballs sweat, smearing his eyeliner.

Small cosmetic changes had been made to the robots in an attempt to unify their look. Some paint here, a red moon there. A few looked as though they wore metal robes complete with welded metal hoods. Decorative ninja stars adorned some torsos, and others had swords welded across their backs.

It was almost as if a giant kid had taken his robot toys and ninja action figures, dropped them into a giant blender, got busted by his giant mom, and had to spend hours gluing them back together. Because giant money doesn't grow on giant trees.

Even Red Moon Clan seemed surprised. Only one lone Moony continued to cheer: a tall, skinny kid who burst into frantic dog barking accompanied by a never-ending fist pump.

"Robots?!" Dagger McJones screamed, surprisingly understandable despite his accent. Sensei Kendu repeated the word in almost perfect mimicry.

"I am afraid that I must also object," Zato said from his position on the platform. "Robots cannot be considered to be your students. They will not be part of the test."

"Aha," Carl said. "They might look like robots, but they are not! Inside these metal shells I give you the finest students the Red Moon Clan has to offer . . .

except for Ping, of course."

"Ting!" Peoni shouted out.

"Yes, of course, Ting," Carl corrected himself. "Behold!"

There was a series of *VRTs*, *WRRRLs*, *CHK-CHNKs*, and *PSSSSSTs* as all the metal monsters cracked open to reveal the Red Moon students inside. They were a grim, angry lot who would have looked at home in a dark back alley. They looked like . . .

"Thugs!" Knight-Lite said. "That guy's Georgi SockHammer, he used to work for the Tick Tock Croc! Night-Knight put him away last summer. And I recognize about half the other guys. They're not ninjas!"

"Please forgive me," Zato said. "I am blind—to confirm what you say I will need to feel their faces."

Zato, looking suddenly frail, stepped off the platform with the help of his sword cane. FangSwan shot out an arm, seemingly to steady the blind man. But Peoni noticed FangSwan pluck a small pouch out of Zato's sleeve and hide it in his own robes.

Zato proceeded to the closest metal monster and put out a hand, feeling the grubby, unshaven face of the man strapped inside. The other faces were very similar, a tapestry of scars, broken noses, and two-day stubble.

"A little old for students," Zato said.

"I'm fifteen. I gots a glandular condition," said the man.

"Unusual, yes," Carl said, "but there are no restrictions on a pupil's age when it comes to ninjas."

"Granted," Zato said.

"In dat case," the man said, "I'm forty-seven and tryin' to betta myself wit valuable job skills."

Zato turned to the Empty Monk. "I humbly put it to you that these suits step across the line. This is not ninja. Remember, your decision today sets a precedent for the future. Please choose wisely."

The Empty Monk turned its basketed head to face Carl.

"They're just tools," Carl said, smiling. "A better, sharper sword . . . that can surf the internet and fire lasers." He winked.

"Allowed," the Empty Monk intoned.

The suits sealed back up and the MechaMoons stood opposite KFA with their rotors whirling and an occasional release of hydraulic pressure. One of them was leaking a small puddle of oil.

Knight-Lite was outraged, at least to the extent that Knight-Lite could be outraged. "Those suits are just stolen from a bunch of low-end superheroes and villains. That one there"—he pointed at an oblong MechaMoon with stubby arms and legs—"that's the Incredible Inedible Egg. It has an exceptionally hard shell and can fire stink bombs loaded with sulfur gas. But I'm pretty sure he retired back in the eighties."

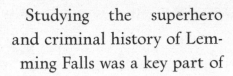

Studying the superhero and criminal history of Lemming Falls was a key part of Knight-Lite's training. He excelled at most everything in the superhero world, except anything that involved actual physical activity. As long as he wasn't swinging on a rope, defusing a bomb, or fighting off a pack of mutant super-warthogs, he was fine. But his knowledge of robots and MechSuits was encyclopedic.

"What about that one?" Peoni asked, pointing at a particularly stylish and sleek-looking suit.

"Oh, that's the Living Lamborghini. A retired Italian race-car driver tried to make a MechSuit out of a one-point-five-million-dollar car. He succeeded, sort of, but never took it adventuring. He was too worried about scratching the paint. I have no idea how the Moonies got it, but those modifications they did are going to lower its Blue Book value."

Knight-Lite pointed out the other suits he knew.

There was KnifeLift: once a humble forklift, it had been torn asunder, sharpened, and rebuilt into a force for evil.

Air Force was a walking jet. It was one of several. They were supposed to be able to transform back and forth between plane and mechbot. Unfortunately they also had a reputation for folding their pilots into origami swans.

There was the hulking metal man-shaped thing that was made for Commander McHuge. McHuge's powers caused him to slowly and constantly grow bigger. By the time they finished building the suit for him he had already outgrown it. The pilot inside looked as though he could reach the controls only for the arms *or* the legs, but not both at the same time.

Several suits looked like different types of construction vehicles: a backhoe, a steamroller, a wrecking ball, and a fairly generic suit with jackhammers for hands. They were all a part of Doctor Worm's Unearthly Engineers. They weren't actually supervillains, just subterranean architects who sometimes crossed paths with the surface world.

Knight-Lite seemed to know the stories behind

them all, but Peoni cut him off as Zato announced the rules.

"Welcome to the Battle Royal," Zato announced, "the third and final challenge of the Test of Three. The rules are simple. Each school has a team. You will fight for your team until you are eliminated. Eliminations occur by leaving the arena, being knocked unconscious, or otherwise being rendered incapable of fighting. Victory is achieved by eliminating all the opposing team's fighters. Questions?"

There were none.

"Good luck. The battle starts in three, two . . ."

Zato's lips had formed the "wha?" shape when a

distant cry caught his ear. From somewhere high over-head came a teeny, tiny voice.

"...so ninja..."

Twin black shapes appeared in the sky over KFA. They quickly grew into two screaming ninjas.

The trick to getting down a mountain quickly isn't really a trick at all—you just need to be willing to jump off at the right place. The trick to surviving the landing is an entirely different and harder feat to accomplish.

Joey and Johnny were hurtling down the moun-tain with their arms spread out. Black wings stretched between their ankles and wrists, making them look like a couple of flying squirrels. Flying squirrels wear-ing ninja hoods and underpants.

WISEMAN NOTE: A shinobifuku, the traditional black, pajama-like outfit of the ninjas, was designed by Ninja Lord Jomon Bloodfist, who liked to do battle and hated formal wear. It was loaded with pockets for concealing weapons, plates of armor, or even skins that could carry liquids—either incoming or outgoing, if you catch my meaning. Bloodfist was a busy man and didn't always have time for bathroom breaks.

The important thing here is that the fuku is mostly made out of two large pieces of fabric. It's how you tie the straps that turns it into proper clothing. At KFA, many spend a whole year struggling to properly wear their uniform, which is why you often see first-year students in outfits resembling black togas.

In time you become one with your ninja uniform. It is the utility knife of the ninja world, and doubles as a hammock, camouflage, a backpack, bandages, a floatation device, a tent, or in this case, makeshift wings.

Joey and Johnny were not flying so much as having a controlled plummet. As they approached the unforgiving ground they threw out grapples, catching the corners of the Red Moon billboard. When the ropes pulled tight there was a tremendous crack and the sign was ripped from its moorings with a groan. It tumbled down the mountain in an explosion of trees and boulders. Flippy valiantly continued to say "I'll see YOU at RED MOON!" until he was splintered against the mountainside.

Joey and Johnny had let go of their grapples just seconds before joining the doomed Red Moon mascot. They hurtled toward the stone wall of their school at a speed that would have seen them splatted, but by twisting their bodies they redirected themselves into a KFA banner. It folded itself around the two boys like a hug and then body-slammed them through the window of

FangSwan's office. There was a terrible symphony of ripping fabric, exploding pottery, and angry chickens.

In a shower of dust and feathers, they burst through another window and slid across five rooftops, leaving a rooster tail of broken tiles spraying into the air behind them. Joey snagged the top of a tree perched on a stone archway, bending it to the point of snapping. Johnny caught Joey's foot and there was a brief, still moment while the tree decided what it was going to do. It decided to give up.

The tree, the stone archway, half a roof, three chickens, and two ninjas tumbled into a dusty heap just yards away from the headmaster's stage. The remains of the KFA banner wafted gently down, settling over the mess.

Everything went still except for a soft cascade of crumbling tiles. Zato and a few Kick Foots took hesitant steps toward Joey and Johnny, but no one wanted to check the heap mercifully covered by the downed banner.

FangSwan drew a breath, preparing to order the custodial staff to fetch garbage bags and shovels.

"Joey?" Peoni said tentatively. "Johnny?"

A gleaming blade poked through the center of the banner and smoothly slid down the length of it. Joey rose from the torn fabric in a two-handed sword stance. Johnny got to his feet behind him, pulling his hammer from nowhere and holding it up in triumph.

"What'd we miss?" Joey asked the assembled crowd.

Johnny, who had been facing the other way, suddenly called out excitedly, "Joey, *Joey!* We get to fight *toasters!*"

EXPLOSIONS AND STUFF

In which the boys will probably jump away
from an explosion in slow motion.

Soga Swifteye might have been the greatest archer the world has ever known. With a single arrow he once managed to depants three samurai, cut the bowstrings of seven rival archers, and kill one duck. All that *and* the arrow landed neatly back in his quiver.

It would've taken a physics professor three chalkboards, two supercomputers, and five headaches to describe all the math involved in making that happen. Soga did it in the blink of an eye, simply for the pleasure of eating one of the emperor's forbidden ducks.

This same ninja was unable to buy a roasting pan, because roasting pans were sold on the second floor of the mall and Soga didn't know how to work an escalator.

For some reason, ninjas and technology just don't mix.

So as the metal monstrosities began to lumber forward, many of the Kick Foots found themselves feeling an unfamiliar sensation. If they still remembered the word for it, they would have called it "fear."

WISEMAN NOTE: Technically, all KFA students knew what fear was. It was a creeping sensation they felt on their scalps whenever FangSwan was near. The feeling was familiar; the source was new.

"Guys . . . ," Joey said. "Remember, inside those invincible suits of armor they're only Moonies." His voice was almost drowned out beneath the heavy thud of mechanical feet.

The shadow from the largest of the mechs fell on FuShoe. She had been preparing for battle by wearing the same pair of socks for a solid two weeks. She felt ready but looked very squishable next to the huge iron foot in front of her.

"FIGHT!" The single word rang out clear and loud in the perfect mimicry of human speech. It was a word the Kick Foots had heard a hundred times and their fear ran away at the sound of it. They leapt into battle, and from the back of the observation platform Sensei Kendu clucked with pleasure.

The huge foot crashed down. FuShoe flipped out of the way and hurled her two steel sais at the Mecha-Moon's windshield. The suit was so big that its pilot had to climb a small ladder if he wanted to control the arms, so blocking the attack was impossible. The sais struck with savage force but bounced harmlessly off the reinforced window. Only halfway up the ladder, the pilot jerked backward reflexively and fell onto the leg controls, making Mecha-McHuge spasm and crash onto his rear end. He rose again, completely undamaged.

The smaller MechaMoon he'd landed on was not so lucky. Its turtle-like shell was dented in the shape of

McHuge's metal butt cheeks and steam was whistling from the cracks that split across its view screen. The unlucky Moony didn't even see FuShoe's foot as it kicked through the broken glass, but he smelled it just fine.

20-19

The opening volley was complete and the Red Moons were down one.

Joey teamed up with Spratt and Whistler to circle a jackhammer mech. It was eight feet tall, made of thick plates of rusting iron, and had the name "BAK-BRAKER" stenciled across its front. Twin exhaust ports issued jets of fire as its powerful, cylindrical arms pounded holes in the arena floor. Spratt and Whistler danced easy circles around it, dodging the blows. Joey leapt onto it from behind and wrapped his hands around the huge rubber hoses that bloomed temptingly from its back.

"Always make sure you have the right tool for the job!" shouted Joey as his katana sliced neatly through the rubber hoses like a . . . well, like a katana through rubber hoses.

There was a loud pop and a hiss as fluid sprayed everywhere. The staccato *BRRRRRRAPTP* of the jackhammer's pummeling arms slowed like a dying heartbeat, eventually *LUB DUB THUMP*ing to a stop. The mech lifted its dead hands with effort and waved them in sad little circles.

Spratt and Whistler each picked a side and sliced the tubes that ran to its legs. As the doomed metal-man tried to take a step forward it slipped in a puddle of its own fluid, toppling like an oversize domino. Powerless, the suit lay facedown on the ground while muffled curses drifted up from inside.

"Practical Advice Guy, right?" said Spratt, holding his hand up to Joey.

"And his tool belt of . . ." They shouted the rest together: "*Well-maintained tools!*" They smacked hands and nearly hugged.

Spratt put an arm on Joey's shoulder and said, "You know, I always kinda thought my dad just made him up!"

"That's what Johnny kept telling me! But he's totally real!"

20–18

WISEMAN NOTE: No, he isn't. But truly staggering coincidences *are* real!

A Kick Foot named Kimberly gave Joey a thumbs-up from across the arena. Her green bandanna was proudly waving in the wind as she stood on the shoulders of what looked like a collection of giant metal toilet-paper tubes with fists and feet. It was still lurching forward, but only because of momentum and habit. Smoke was spewing from the hole where its head used to be.

20–17

"Behind you!" Joey shouted. He pointed wildly to a spot just behind Kim. The girl thought Joey was pointing at her and made a little victory bow back at Joey. So the wrecking ball took her completely by surprise as it walloped her out of the arena and through the south wall of the astronomy building.

19–17

A MechaMoon wielding a wrecking ball extended a single arm high above the arena. It moved ponderously through the battling ninjas on huge, stable treads. The Moony controlling it sat inside a cab enclosed with metal and glass. It looked like a crane—I mean *exactly* like a crane! It was definitely just a crane. You'd think someone would've noticed that before now.

"Wheeeeee! Joey, you have got to try this!" Johnny was gripping the giant wrecking ball with his legs, letting it sling him through the battlefield while he picked targets to thump with his hammer.

The Moony inside the crane frantically

struggled with the controls, trying to shake Johnny free. The ball swung more and more erratically, heedless of friend or foe—a ton and a half of metal tetherball in a game of round-the-world.

Whipping fast and low, the wrecking ball knocked a ring-shaped MechaMoon end over end, toppling it to the very edge of the arena. Landing on its side, it swiveled a great tusked head in Johnny's direction and fired its trunk-like cannon at him. The recoil sent it sliding across the arena and into the crowd.

Knight-Lite pointed excitedly. "That's the Mastodonut! He was a member of the Dinosaucers along with Frizzbeast, Tiresaurus Rex, TriceraTop, and Hula Hippo!"

"What was a hippo doing in a dino-themed supergroup?" asked Peoni.

"Honestly, I think the whole circular-dinosaur theme was a bit of a stretch, never mind the hippo."

"Well, I wonder why the Empty Monk hasn't counted him out yet," Peoni said, looking over at the basket-headed monk. "Everyone can see he was knocked out of bounds."

Mastodonut had rolled back to a standing position amid a small pile of groaning Red Moon students. Lowering his tusks, he began charging toward the arena. Before the rampaging donut could make it more than a few feet, dozens of daggers suddenly blossomed from his back like acupuncture needles. Each knife was perfectly placed, and Mastodonut's cylindrical body arched backward and fell, crushing its trunk into a child's drawing of an accordion.

Back on the stage, Professor McJones rocked back and forth on his heels whistling a pleasant Irish ballad. His coat jangled quite a bit less than it had moments before. The Empty Monk threw the black flag of disqualification at the downed MechaMoon almost as an afterthought.

19–16

"Johnny, stop playing and help us!" Joey screamed, ducking under an iron rod that was glowing red-hot.

"Joey, I want to keep him! I'm gonna call him Swingy SmashenBash!" Johnny said.

"JOHNNY!"

"Oh, fine," sighed Johnny.

People think martial arts are all about punching through walls with your face and catching throwing stars with chopsticks . . . and they're absolutely right. But they're also about making your opponent use his own energy against himself.

Johnny leapt down toward the cab of the crane, landing like a cat. He knocked on the roof. "All your tattoos are misspelled!" he said to the man inside.

The man, whose left arm said "Muthar" and whose

right arm said "No feer," made another bad decision and aimed the wrecking ball directly at himself.

Johnny landed on the ground and watched the crumpled remains of the crane overbalance at the edge of the arena and then topple down the mountain, destroying a twenty-foot-wide chunk of the arena's wall on its way down.

"Good-bye, Swingy," Johnny said, looking at the smoking hole. "I'll miss you."

19–15

The mech known as NumberONE Fan scuttled about on a pair of stunted legs, its enormous rotating blades deflecting every attack thrown at it. It had blown a sturdy Kick Foot named Jo Jo to the very edge of the arena's boundary. The basket-headed monk stood ready with its black flag as the ninja fought the pummeling, hurricane-force winds. Jo Jo threw a grappling hook onto the mech itself, but he found his grip weakening. Five fingers held on to the rope, then four fingers, three, two . . . none.

"I am a leaf in the wind," said Jo Jo to himself. It was true, but he was an autumn leaf and the wind is not kind to autumn leaves. He was blown out of bounds and through FangSwan's only remaining unbroken window. The chickens, still angry from Joey and Johnny's intrusion, took out their vengeance on Jo Jo's unconscious body.

18–15

So far this had been fun, Joey admitted to himself. A little scary, but less so than most days at KFA. They were even doing well, and he still had his secret weapon, an ace up his sleeve in the form of Knight-Lite's mech-wrecker.

Joey had been on fire, but only briefly. It was out now, and he managed to use the smoke to screen his movements so that he came up behind the Living

Lamborghini, the only MechaMoon that was even faster than the Kick Foots. A hard spinning kick caused the Moony's laser to miss his intended target.

The shot hit the Inedible Egg suit and it spun angrily. Pulling its arms close, it rolled in the weebling-wobbling manner of eggs and punched the Lamborghini in the chest.

"What's the big idea?!" the egg-man yelled.

"It was the kid!" But he got no farther. The punch had caused some belt to shift inside the Living Lamborghini. An unseen chain reaction rocked through its frame, ending in a grinding squeal as its chest plate popped open and smoke billowed out.

18–14

"Useless foreign cars," complained the egg.

The egg rolled toward Joey. Joey was waving his sword in complicated patterns and naming each sword stance out loud.

"Dragon Bathes in the Sun," he said, spreading an arm and pointing the sword tip skyward. Then he swept the sword low across the ground. "Tiger Swims Annoyed," he intoned.

"Cute dance, kid, but you ain't gonna pierce this shell!" said the egg.

"Ninja Distracts a Moron," said Joey.

"What was that?" said the egg.

Johnny's hammer connected to the back of the egg with a *CLANG* so loud that a flock of parrots on an island three hundred miles away added the word "clang" to their vocabulary.

As the ringing faded, both boys could hear the Moony inside bouncing back and forth off the egg's unbreakable shell. He eventually came to a stop, and the MechaMoon slowly fell over and did not move.

"Beautifully done, Johnny."

"Hmm. He weebled, wobbled, and fell down, Joey. I didn't think that was possible!"

18–13

Joey stared at the tip of his sword with a questioning eye. It was moving against his will, slowly turning out and to the right.

"Johnny, do you see this?" The moment the words left his mouth, his sword left his hand. It spun end over end across the battlefield.

Johnny clapped in delight. "That," he said, "was a great trick."

"No trick," Joey said. "Trouble."

The two schools had rallied, regrouping on opposite sides of the arena. The MechaMoon that had once been Air Force stood apart from the others. Twin hatches opened and an enormous red and silver "U" rose up out of its back. It was the biggest magnet the boys had ever seen. Heavy cables of different lengths and thicknesses ran to a little square MechaMoon, which was vibrating and sparking with power.

The electromagnet was making a deep thrum, and the air around it was blurry and distorted. Swords, daggers, and shuriken were getting torn out of pockets and belts. Several Kick Foots refused to let go of their weapons and found themselves getting dragged across the field.

Bolts began to loosen from the stands holding the noncombatants, tumbling the first three rows of Moony spectators onto the field. Zippers and buckles were ripped from their clothes. It was a bad day for wearing studded shoulder pads and a worse one for ear- and nose rings. On the judge's stage, Dagger McJones held his coat closed and took a few steps back.

In seconds the magnet on top of Air Force was bristling with ninja weapons and Moony tech of every sort.

"We have all your weapons," came a booming voice over the loudspeakers on Mecha-McHuge. The Kick Foots stood in a loose circle, looking uncomfortable. Some of them patted their pockets hoping to find something to continue the fight with. "Surrender and we'll make this as painless as possible. By which I mean, still fairly painful."

A cold whistling wind howled across the battlefield.

Joey stepped forward with his empty hands open. "Wood isn't magnetic," he said to the mech.

"Um . . . yeah, so?"

"It means you didn't get ALL our weapons. . . ."

Johnny was in midleap and his hammer had an aura of fire around it like a spaceship reentering earth's atmosphere. Johnny didn't say a word; the hammer spoke for them both.

And it said, "*Ker-THOOOOM!*"

The impact drove the magnet down into Air Force's chest cavity while the rippling shock wave knocked everyone in the arena off their feet. The stolen weapons fountained into the air.

18–12

A race ensued. The Kick Foots rushed forward to reclaim their weaponry while the MechaMoons tried to cut them off. A low, squat mech stood guard, squirting streams of purple liquid from a hose on its arm. The huge tank strapped to his back was stamped with a dark purple octopus.

Spratt took a face full of octo-toxin and fell bonelessly to the ground.

Whistler snatched up a throwing knife

and hurled it into the spout, instantly stopping the flow of purple poison. He paused for a victory fist pump and was snagged by a clawed arm and thrown out of bounds, landing with a groan just behind the teachers' podium.

16–12

Mecha-McHuge popped open a hatch on his knees, revealing a bristling array of rockets. He carefully selected a target. "Time to push the GAME OVER button," he declared to himself, and fired.

Meanwhile, the man inside the suit, called Octo-Squirt by his fellow Moonies, had been having a bad fight. The mech was slow as a sloth and smelled like old ham. The tank of octo-toxin he was lugging around sloshed unsteadily, making him stumble and trip. Until recently, every time he made it to an active part of the arena the fight had moved somewhere else. He was hot and cramped, and someone had switched his drinking water with Diet Mister Pib. He hated Diet Mister Pib.

A light flashed on his view screen, indicating an incoming missile. He didn't even know he had a light for that . . .

FABOOOSH!

16–11

A vast cloud of octo-toxin mushroomed up from the smoking rubble and settled like a purple dome over the arena. It covered Kick Foots and MechaMoons alike.

The MechaMoons were sealed inside airtight suits and were mostly unaffected. Only the MechaMoon known as Crush-Dozer succumbed to the toxin. His pre–Battle Royal breakfast had consisted of beans, garlic, and pork, so he'd kept his windows down.

The cloud's effect was devastating. Trimil made a desperate attempt to save his girlfriend, Mai-Fan. Using all his strength, he grabbed her just before the rocket hit and threw her high into the air. The purple cloud bloomed beneath her as she flipped and tumbled and managed to come down out of bounds, but safe.

The Empty Monk threw down a black flag to disqualify her. Mai-Fan picked it up, tied it around her nose, and dove back into the cloud for Trimil. It did no good and she quickly succumbed to the purple vapors, collapsing in a heap beside the unconscious body of her boyfriend.

0–10

"No, NO, NO!" Peoni yelled in the moment of silence that followed. Knight-Lite looked down and shifted his eyes about nervously. They both knew about octo-toxin firsthand.

The Empty Monk stared and listened intently. The seconds passed with only the sound of hydraulic motors and metal feet moving in the purple haze. One after another the remaining MechaMoons exited the cloud and stood in a loose ring as it slowly dissipated in the breeze.

Finally the monk reached inside its robes and threw the red flag into the remains of the swirling purple cloud. Red Moon had won. Carl Crescent turned to FangSwan with his best victorious-but-gracious face on. FangSwan had not turned away from the arena.

"Excuse me, but I think you dropped something," came a voice from the cloud.

Two figures appeared as silhouettes in the thinning

fog. Joey and Johnny walked to its edge. Johnny was holding the red flag.

"Impossible!" said the Empty Monk, showing uncharacteristic emotion. Johnny tossed the weighted flag back at its stunned, basketed head.

"But—but that's a cloud of octo-toxin!" It was Sensei Renbow who spoke, but everyone was thinking the same thing.

"Yeah," said Johnny, taking a deep inhale, "smells like sunshine and circus peanuts!"

Joey stared down Carl Crescent. "Nice try, but we've been drinking from the source. Now, if you'll excuse us, I believe we've got a Battle Royal to win."

2–10

CRUSHING DEFEAT

In which someone goes home crying.

"**A**re you regretting your bravado?" Johnny asked. "I'm regretting your bravado!"

Now the only thing Joey and Johnny had time for was to stay one step ahead of the onslaught of lasers, tasers, phasers, and flamethrowers aimed at them. It certainly was a lot easier fighting the MechaMoons when they had more targets.

In the background, NumberONE Fan was using his winds to push the Kick Foot students out of bounds in the unlikely event of their waking up. He'd once spent a summer doing lawn care, and this was just like using a leaf-blower. It was nice to feel useful.

"What about the thing?" Johnny said, ducking between the legs of a big metal spider-centaur.

"What thing?" Joey asked, perching for a moment on the bubble head of the claw machine, causing it to scrape at its own face in an attempt to grab him.

"The thing that you haven't been using," Johnny yelled. "*That* thing!"

Oh, that thing. Joey wondered himself why he had left the brass disks up his sleeves. It made sense to use them. Hadn't he pulled them out three times during the fight, only to put them back again? All he had to do was clap them together and this fight would be over . . . in theory. Or he might become Joey, the armless ninja.

"Ooh, that's Dreidel, the Jewish superhero," Knight-Lite said as Joey and Johnny ducked the whirling arms of a MechaMoon whose lower body was a spinning top. "Or at least he was before he retired. From everything I read, it was a pretty potent suit of armor."

"Why'd he retire?" Peoni asked and grimaced as Johnny went tumbling. He fell over the edge of the arena but managed to catch the wall with the head of his hammer.

"Oh," said Knight-Lite, "he did great for a while, but then his rogues' gallery got together and decided to commit crimes only on the Sabbath. After that, he didn't see the point. I had heard the suit was in a museum."

While the Dreidel mech watched Johnny's near-death experience, Joey lunged, wedging the tip of his sword just above the whirling top. There was a metal hiccup and suddenly the bottom went still while the robot's torso turned into a spinning blur. It fell on its side and skittered around for a while before coming to a merciful stop. From inside there was the sound of someone being messily sick.

2-9

Joey and Johnny were doing surprisingly well against the nine remaining MechaMoons, playing defense in an attempt to drain power supplies, expend ammunition, and find weaknesses. It was a good plan, but it was a two-way street. Joey and Johnny were exhausted, Joey was out of shuriken, and deep in the back of their minds they both knew that the Moonies needed to get lucky only once.

WISEMAN NOTE: Twice! There were two of them.

So when McHuge yelled *"Stop!"* the boys thankfully grabbed a breather, backed shoulder to shoulder in the middle of the MechaMoons.

"Let's end this!" McHuge boomed.

"Yes!" Peoni screamed. "Joey, what are you doing? End this!" She was clapping her hands together in his direction, but it wasn't applause. It was a suggestion. Joey thought about the disks again. He could end this in a clap.

"Which of you is the leader?" McHuge asked.

"I am," both boys said at the same time.

"No, I am!" they continued, staring at each other from over their shoulders.

"Johnny," Joey said, "let me be the leader, okay?"

Johnny grunted, and Joey took it as a yes.

"I am," Joey declared.

"Sort of," Johnny said under his breath.

The mechs had stopped attacking and backed away to form a line in the middle of the arena. McHuge stood in the center. If Joey looked carefully, he could just see the pilot's face inside the mech's red windscreen.

"I am the leader of the MechaMoons," he announced.

"Congratulations," said Joey, leaning on his knees for just a moment to take in a gasping breath. "Sounds like you got the best prize in the cereal box!"

"Face me in single combat. If you win, we'll power down. If I win, your buddy surrenders. Either way, this is over!"

Joey looked up at the nearly twenty-foot-tall mech with its heavy metal plating. Those arms would never get tired; its lungs weren't burning. Joey had watched nearly every one of his fellow combatants deliver pulverizing blows to the monster and it had suffered nothing worse than superficial damage to its Red Moon logo. Now it said "Red Moo."

Joey attempted to point menacingly at him, but the effect was ruined by coughing. "I'm gonna . . . I'm gonna punch the *Red* off you and then you'll just say *Moo!*"

"Uh, what?" said McHuge.

Johnny gave him a funny look. "Joey, you can still play leader, but maybe let me make the threats."

"What's it gonna be, boy? You and I can end this quick or you can go down slow!" Steam hissed as he punched his car-size fists together. "It won't make a difference to me!"

Joey looked at his hands and then turned his head to Johnny. What could be more ninja than one lone man against a hulking metal giant for the fate of the world? Johnny looked back fiercely and shook his head no.

"I'll do it!" Joey said. If needed, he still had his secret weapon.

Under his breath, Johnny growled, "You are the *worst* leader!"

The MechaMoons closed in like a wall as Mecha-McHuge took one long step toward Joey.

"NO!" cried Sensei Renbow. "I've told you a thousand times, *the shark doesn't shake hands.*"

Joey stood his ground as the mech lumbered forward. In his head a lonely French horn played while he pictured the movie that would almost certainly be made of this moment. First a long shot of the two warriors, then an intense close-up on their eyes. First of Joey, then of his enemy. Cut to a shot of the sun rising over the mountain. Perhaps a sped-up film of a plant in bloom! Then an eagle crying out as it passes overhead. Quick, something abstract: A small lizard runs across a flat stone! A dewdrop in midfall!

With all his attention on the titan in front of him,

Joey began to run, his sword held in both hands and a slight limp in his right leg.

"Now," said Mecha-McHuge.

The Power Generator mech had been trying to stay clear of battle. She wasn't really made to fight, just to store lots of power. Already some of this power was leaking out in blue sparks and lightning flashes. The energy inside Genny was begging to be released either by a lucky strike on her dented hull or through the metal rod that was pointed right at Joey.

At McHuge's word, a fat, zigzagging line of blue-white light erupted from the end of the generator's rod. Sound split the mountaintop as if someone had ripped the sky in half. The deadly serpent of energy hurtled toward Joey, whose entire focus was on McHuge.

"Pancakes!" Johnny yelled, leaping hammer-first into the bolt of blue fire.

Light crackled around Johnny. His body jerked as the power surged through him, and he landed with a graceless, smoking thump on the ground behind the

MechaMoons. He rolled end over end across the arena floor, coming to a stop just short of the outer edge. Tiny blue arcs of electricity sparked from him, making his body continue to jerk.

Across the arena, Genny sparked one final time and went black and silent.

"Now. Use it *now!*" screamed Zato.

Peoni and Knight-Lite shot a glance at their vice principal and then back at Joey, who stood motionless, in shock. His sword was on the ground at his feet and he was looking down at his sleeves.

"Do it, Joey!" whispered Peoni.

"It's all over now, boy," McHuge said, looking taller than ever.

Joey was alone and looked tiny in the shadow of the looming mech. The line of remaining Mecha-Moons began to close in. They could've easily finished him, but instead they tittered and laughed, celebrating his despair as much as their assured victory. They could take their time crushing this boy. This is exactly what makes bad men bad. Anyone can do bad things, but only the wicked get pleasure from the pain they cause.

Joey let the brass disks slide into his hands. It was only fair—he was leveling the playing field. Without their machines the Moonies would be nothing. Distantly he could hear Peoni and Knight-Lite urging him to activate the device. Even Johnny had told him to use it. Joey himself had been the one who insisted on having it. He looked at the bright brass disks with their shiny red buttons. All over with a clap of his hands.

Joey looked down between those two hands and saw a third. It was the hand of Headmaster FangSwan pressed forever into the center stone of the arena. The hand was smaller than his own, and alone ... and empty.

Joey let the disks fall, spinning and glinting as they tumbled to the earth. He pulled his eyes off the handprint in the stone and stared at the surrounding MechaMoons. Not at them, but through them.

He took a deep breath and began to speak:

"Well, this is the end for Joey and his stalwart friend Johnny!" Joey announced loudly. The Moonies paused their approach and twisted their heads to look at one another.

"Know this, you villainous hordes, though I, *Joey*, shall dispatch hundreds—*nay, thousands*—of you before I expire, those of you who survive shall have the noble honor of telling the last of our exalted exploits!"

Joey gestured to the MechaMoons, and then, turning his back to them, he addressed the gathered students and teachers from both schools, his words growing more passionate with every breath.

"And now, the call to arms! We rush forth unto doom's bosom! Chop! Slice! And alas, I fall! Fall! Fall!"

The last words were shouted while Joey sank to his knees.

"Those your famous last words, boy?" McHuge asked, his foot in stomping position.

Joey rose lightly to his feet. "No," he said. "They're just words. I'm not dying with a B minus."

Snatching his sword off the ground, Joey ran up McHuge's slow-moving body. Inside, the pilot cursed and scrambled up the ladder to the arm controls. The massive limbs lifted to squash Joey like a bug, but not fast enough. The young ninja flew skyward and pushed from the tip of the mech's upraised fist, jumping as high as his bruised body would allow. He hung twirling in the air for a moment and then dove toward the ground, sword first. A cloud of powdered rock erupted from the shattering impact.

The other MechaMoons had backed out of the way. When the smoke cleared, they saw Joey crouched in the center of the arena, his katana embedded into the ground halfway to the hilt. It had struck deep in the hand-print of FangSwan. Exactly between the lines of life and fate.

McHuge had fallen back, but he sat up on his elbows. The pilot was laughing as he grabbed the microphone. "You missed? After all that, you missed?"

Joey pushed himself away from his sword and pointed up.

A shadow against the sun was falling toward earth. The shape was ragged and a little crispy around the edges, but it was still Johnny. The hammer came down as big as the moon and it pounded into the back of Joey's sword. The resulting thunderclap finished the job Joey had started. A network of cracks radiated from the sword buried deep in the stone.

"Boom," Johnny said, standing next to Joey.

The cracks deepened and lengthened as they stretched across the battlefield, the ground rumbling and shifting. It felt as if the whole mountain was shaking. The tear in the stone extended in zips and breaks until it bisected the entire arena: Red Moon on one side, the two remaining Kick Foots on the other. Two young ninjas finished what FangSwan had begun thirty years ago when he struck the center stone.

"Ut oh," said McHuge, looking at the ground crumbling beneath his feet. He and the rest of the Moonies were standing on the half of the arena that hung over empty space. They had just enough time to wave good-bye before gravity noticed what was going on and eagerly gobbled them up.

After the sounds of avalanche died out, the crowd stood in stunned silence. Even the Empty Monk's basketed head held an expression of disbelieving awe. No one knew it yet, but Joey and Johnny had just won the Battle Royal.

25

EPILOGUE
In which frustrating questions
go entirely unanswered.

There was a rush of students, a cheering crowd, and Joey and Johnny were lifted onto shoulders like conquering heroes. The well-wishers bounced and threw the boys into the air and then hurried off the arena floor because the whole thing was a death trap. Chunks of rock large and small occasionally dropped off to join their brethren far below. Once on solid ground, the Kick Foots began rejoicing anew. Even the teachers joined in.

Peoni couldn't make up her mind. She wanted to kiss them. She wanted to hit them, or at least hit Joey. Giving in to the moment, she decided to do one now and the other later. When she reached the boys, she too was lifted into the air and the school celebrated their *three* champions.

"Why didn't you?" she asked Joey. They both knew what she was referring to.

"It wasn't *ninja*," he said.

While Peoni was almost in tears with relief, Knight-Lite was openly sobbing. His days as a side-kick had brought plenty of experience with being helpless in the face of life-or-death situations. He had spent far more time tied to a chair as a hostage than he ever did fighting actual crime. Today he discovered that he dealt with the stress far better when it was *his* life in danger, which says something about his kind heart.

A ripple rolled across the crowd. Wherever it passed the cheers stilled and the party stopped. The students parted around a figure that was almost glowing white. Amid all the day's events and destruction, FangSwan's dress robes had remained pristine and pressed. He had come to address the two champions.

"You," FangSwan said, "and you."

"Yes, Headmaster?" both boys said eagerly.

"You broke my school." FangSwan's jade eyes flicked to the ragged edge of the devastated arena and back to Joey and Johnny.

"Yes, sir. Sorry, sir!" they chimed together.

"Fix it," he said and walked away. And that was the

last he spoke of their victory, although the following morning pancakes were back on the menu.

There was a price to pay for losing. The Red Moon Clan would now have to be . . . ninjas. Only this time, they had to be *real* ninjas. No more stolen, broken, or borrowed technology. No more jet boots or Mech-Suits. No more cross promotions or corporate retreats. Just swords, toe socks, and ninjutsu.

Over the months to come, their numbers would drop. Those with questionable morals would drift into henching for one or more of the many supervillains who made their home in Lemming Falls. Others found safer career paths, like lion proctologist or professional train puncher.

Those who remained were going to have to start with the basics. They would fumble and fail, and for a long while they were going to be terrible. They were going to be a joke, but in time some of them might actually become ninjas.

Just, you know, don't hold your breath.

Ting had not been seen since his victory in the Duel of Champions. At Peoni's request, Vice Principal Zato led a group of teachers to find their missing friend. They had little trouble storming the Red Moon headquarters, where a terrified Moony named Humphrey told them Ting was being held in time-out until his loyalties were determined. Much to everyone's surprise, when the doors to his cell were opened Ting was gone. All that was left behind was a single piece of paper with the words "I QUIT" written below a picture of Flippy the Ninja making a rude gesture. It was Ting's best drawing yet.

Rumors speak of him walking the world and doing great deeds. Others suggest he's on a quest to find Brad. But for now, his whereabouts remain unknown.

Speaking of Brad, the school had three champions, but the biggest buzz revolved around their only loss. Was he alive or dead? Everyone had seen him sacrifice himself to save Ting, but there had been some unusual details. There was no body, and while ninjas are known for disappearing, they don't normally disappear in an eye-damaging splash of purple light. Brad's fate had become an enigma. Strangest of all, Joey had become his strongest advocate.

"Of *course* he's not dead!" Joey would complain. "He's Brad!"

"You might be right," Knight-Lite agreed. "Gosh! That almost-ultraviolet glow right before he disappeared reminded me of Peek-A-Boo Dingo." The sidekick waited to see if anyone knew what he was talking about. They didn't, so he carried on. "Australian superhero? He can teleport short distances and he's a master of Australian head-to-head combat. Sometimes went by the name Blink Dog. . . . Ringing any bells?"

Three pairs of eyes stared back. At least Peoni smiled in a supportive way. Johnny's brow furrowed and he rubbed his forehead as he contemplated a martial art made entirely of head-butts.

"See," Joey said. "Teleported, not dead."

"Of course, that was a lot more power than Dingo ever used," Knight-Lite said, "but I guess that could mean he teleported far away."

"Exactly," Joey said. He pointed at Knight-Lite as if he was a star witness for the defense. "Like Florida!"

Knight-Lite knew the next thing he had to say wouldn't make anyone happy. But the information had already cued up in his brain and the only way he knew to get rid of it was through his mouth.

". . . or out into space, the bottom of the ocean, into a solid object, the earth's core," he continued in a sad, regretful tone, "and there's also the possibility that he's in a different dimension altogether."

"Like a universe where the world is populated by giant snails?" Johnny asked.

"That is one possibility," Knight-Lite said. "I guess."

"So what you're saying is—" Peoni started.

"Brad would have super speed and be able to defeat anyone with his nunchucks made of saltshakers!" Johnny declared.

"What he's saying is," Joey said, "we don't know. But this is Brad. If there's anyone in the school—*in the world*—who can cheat death, it's Brad!"

This argument was repeating itself all over campus. Students and teachers alike found themselves landing on one side of the debate or the other, sometimes switching their positions so quickly they'd find themselves changing sides midargument.

Was Brad dead?

In the quad, the pillar normally used for notes and announcements filled with ink-brush drawings of his face, or calligraphic writings of his name left not in memorial, but rather in hope. Less than a day after the first note was placed, the pillar had been transformed into a tree with foliage made of paper leaves.

Carl Crescent fled Kick Foot and Red Moon alike, but not before FangSwan forced the regional branch manager to chew him a new statue. In an unusual show of kind spirits and generosity, KFA's headmaster commissioned the statue out of soap.

WISEMAN NOTE: This is probably because he wanted an actual statue instead of a pile of broken teeth. Not much was known about FangSwan's limitations, but he certainly knew much about the limitations of others.

In time he presented the four-by-eight-foot carving to the assembled group of students. It did *not* look like a lion. It was definitely a quadruped, and it probably had a head. There was a large, bulbous lump that seemed to form into some kind of . . . mouth? Over here something that might be an eye, or an ear. What was probably meant to be the main body swelled toward the back, narrowed, and then ballooned again into what should have been shoulders. It looked a little like a hippo with a toupee, a little like a bear wrestling with an inflatable raft, and entirely like penance.

FangSwan was disturbingly proud of it, to the point of being chatty, even with the students.

"Come. Come close, look at this texture," he said. "You can see the teeth marks!

"Over here." FangSwan hooked a finger at a student too scared to move. "He must've softened the soap with his spit, because he really got a nice big chunk out.

"If you taste this paw you would think it tastes like soap. NO!" He licked his finger and lightly rubbed the lumpy shape, bringing it back to his tongue and tasting with the palette of a connoisseur. "It is *salty!*" Fang-Swan smiled. "From all the tears."

It is oddly comforting to know that even at his happiest, FangSwan still breeds nightmares.

It was months before anyone saw Carl Crescent again. His mustache was gone, his hair was cut, and he called himself PopStar Pete. Knight-Lite had caught a clip of him on TwitFace selling some kind of energy drink he claimed could grant you superpowers.

This was more his element—selling soda suited him. He looked happy and betrayed a hint of his former life only when he said, "LightSpeed PopStar Pete says try our New Night Ninja Neon. A flavor so silent, it's deadly!"

Always eloquent, Carl had stuttered—just a little—on the word "ninja."

"And how is your secret mission coming along?" Zato asked Peoni.

Peoni looked uncomfortable. "There are too many rules, and you need to time everything perfectly. I just can't do it, Vice Principal."

"Of course you can, and I need not remind you of its importance."

Zato sat at his chair, and for the first time Peoni noticed that the high back was not carved with a dragon as she had always thought. The twisting neck was made of two earthworms. The claws belonged to moles. The wings, a great bat. The head was that of a toothy, jawed fish found only in the blackest depths of the ocean. All of them were creatures that got by without the use of their eyes. A blind man would touch the chair and then he would know each of them for what they were. Only a sighted man would be tricked into thinking it was a dragon.

"I don't think I'm the right girl for the job," she said.

"Perhaps you have a point about timing," Zato said. "Maybe you could use a little help, and I know just who to ask."

In the celebrations (for some) and shame (for others) that followed, no one had noticed the Empty Monk slipping away. It walked unmolested down the mountain to the gondola station and rode back into Lemming Falls. From there it walked to a parking garage and was met by a huge black limousine. A wall of a man unfolded himself from the front seat and opened the rear door. The Empty Monk sat down and lifted the basket off its head. Safe and alone, the Empty Monk could once again be the shadow man.

"Mr. Slab, privacy screen up, if you please." A click

and the opaque glass slid up, separating the front of the limo from the back. The shadow man knew the limo was completely soundproof. He had specified that when it was built.

A deep breath pulled past clenched teeth, and then he screamed, "I hate ninjas!"

The volume of his own voice filled the car and hurt his ears. A minute passed as his breathing and heart rate returned to normal. His hand reached out to a small control panel and pressed the COMM button.

"Thank you, Mr. Slab." The privacy screen came back down. He pressed a second button and paused while the connection was made.

"How did things go, sir?" asked a pleasant, albeit mechanical, female voice.

"Not well," the shadow man said. "My whole plan to drive FangSwan mad, ruined by a couple of ninjas." He shrugged out of the monk's stiff robes, making them, for the first time, truly empty. Underneath he wore an expensive and ugly business suit.

"And Red Moon, sir?"

"Cut all funding. Fire the PR team," he said. He pulled out a cigar and brought a metallic hand to his face. A small flame danced out of its thumb. "We're going to shift those resources to the EYEball project. List it under private security."

"Very good, sir."

The shadow man eased back in his comfortable bucket seat, the large circular saw at the end of his right arm doing further damage to the once-fine leather. A third button was pressed and several small projectors focused a three-dimensional image of Joey and Johnny in the center of the cab.

The shadow man was at long last illuminated by the slowly rotating image. He was a broad man with hardened features. A very old and thick scar ran down the side of his face, sketching a line across his left eye. It gave that eye a bulging, dangerous look.

"Well, it seems even a pawn can upset a king. Congratulations, boys, you've earned the personal attention of Scar EyeFace.

"Io," he said. "Get me all the information you can on Joey and Johnny, the ninjas."

Kevin Serwacki was born in Nairobi, Kenya, deep in the heart of the jungle. His path as a writer was set when his illustrated essay titled "Kevin's Waves and Boats" was given an A and posted on the refrigerator door. The showing was a stellar success, and soon Kevin's empire dominated the refrigerator and had spread to the downstairs guest bathroom. He sits in a swivel chair, overlooking the city. There are other refrigerator doors and other guest bathrooms, and soon they shall be *his*. . . .

Chris Pallace is a dad, husband, writer, game designer, professional artist, amateur cook, and intermediate juggler. His own father once observed: there's the Easy Way, the Hard Way, and the Chris Way. The Chris Way intends to be easier than the Easy Way, but is almost always harder than the Hard Way. While admitting that that is true, Chris would like to point out that it is the journey he enjoys.

Kevin and **Chris** work together, making giant sculptures and little doors at their art studio, the Blue Toucan, in Rochester, New York.